BLOOD
& WINE

M | Independently Published

Edited by Kathleen Payne

ISBN: 9798488256682

"For this moment, this one moment, we are together. I press you to me. Come, pain, feed on me. Bury your fangs in my flesh. Tear me asunder."

— Virginia Woolf, *The Waves*

1

MARIAH

I meet my father for the first time at the Shenandoah Valley Airport. I don't recognize him, which isn't surprising given that the only photo I've seen of him is a somewhat blurry polaroid taken almost twenty years ago.

"Mariah," he says, holding his hand out for me to shake. "It's good to finally meet you."

"Yeah, you, too..." I shake his hand and shift my denim backpack onto my opposite shoulder.

I have no idea what to call this man. Dad isn't an option, so I guess that leaves me with...Ed? Edward? Mr. Radcliff?

"Call me Edward," he says, for which I'm grateful.

I drag my suitcase off the conveyor belt and follow him into the bright mid-day sun. He unlocks his car—a sleek red Ferrari that probably costs more than the house I grew up in. I'm convinced my bulky bag won't fit in the sportscar's trunk, but he tilts and rotates my suitcase until it slides in easily, like a magic trick.

Ducking into the car's posh interior, I immediately feel underdressed in my ripped jeans, Nirvana tee shirt, and my grandpa's old red-checkered flannel. With only a single row of seats, I'm forced to sit beside Edward instead of in my preferred spot behind the driver where I can lip sync to my music in peace. I'll have to resort to more subtle measures to sidestep the impending awkwardness.

I fish around in my backpack for my CD player.

"Feel free to take a nap," Edward says. "You must be tired from traveling."

I nod because I *am* tired, but not from traveling. The flight from Baltimore wasn't long at all. However, the past year has been a non-stop nightmare that I can't seem to wake up from.

My mom was diagnosed with ovarian cancer barely a month into my senior year of high school. I begged her to let me take time off from school to help take care of her. Having skipped ninth grade, I was already way ahead of schedule, but my mom wouldn't have it. So, instead of slowing down, I sped up. Worked myself to the bone to graduate in one semester instead of two, with honors.

Not being a full-time student gave me the flexibility to become her primary caretaker when things worsened. I took a part-time job working at a music store, but outside those few hours, my entire life revolved around making sure she ate enough calories and drank enough water when swallowing all those horse pills.

A couple of weeks before she died, she came into my room and handed me a first-class plane ticket totally out of the blue.

"Why am I going to Virginia?" I asked her.

"You're going to see your father after I'm gone."

There was no way I'd heard her correctly. My absent father had never so much as sent me a birthday card. I checked the date of the flight, and my blood ran cold as I realized what the date implied. She knew when she was going to die, in the way she knew about everything else before it happened.

My mother was clairvoyant. It was one of her gifts, like her ability to communicate with ghosts. She always said the latter was more of a curse than a talent. Much like a line in a song that gets stuck in your head, dead people can be super annoying.

"Does my father want me to visit? I mean, he's never even tried to meet me."

"I wrote him a letter explaining the situation," she said. "The ticket was his response."

"Okay, but...shouldn't I get a say in this?"

She laughed cheerlessly, adjusting the purple scarf around her head.

"Wouldn't that be something," she said, in the way that meant, *I've already seen it happen, so there's no point in us fighting about it.* "Think of it as your chance to visit the house where I grew up."

Mom always talked about the house she grew up in like it was the most enchanted place on earth. Her great-grandfather had purchased the hundred-acre estate back in the twenties, and it'd stayed in the family until the late seventies, when my grandpa sold it to Edward Radcliff—my father.

I've wanted to visit my family's old estate since I was a little girl. I just always figured Mom and I would go see it together.

"Please put the ticket somewhere safe," she said. "I'm going to take a bath."

"Give me a minute. I'll come help you."

"Don't bother, sweetheart." She waved her hand. "I've seen my final moments, and they don't involve cracking my head open in the shower. But hey, who knows, I could be wrong for once."

Even now, I can hear her humorless laughter trailing down the hallway.

It's been three weeks since she died, and ever since, I feel like I'm walking around with a hole in my chest that's only getting bigger.

"It won't take long to reach the vineyard," Edward says.

"Sweet." I adjust the width of my headphones, rest the foam pads over my ears, and press play on my CD player. Within seconds, I'm nodding along to the lilting melody of "Dreams" by The Cranberries while gazing absently at fields of dry corn stalks shorn at the ankles like hairs on a boy's buzzed head.

I crack the window, letting the wind fan my dark, bone-straight hair around my face. My hair is one of many traits I'm glad to have inherited from my mom. When I was little, getting to play with her dark-brown waves was my second-favorite reward for finishing all my chores, a packet of Pop Rocks being the ultimate prize. The hair loss had to have been the roughest leg of her chemotherapy journey. It totally sucked—the nausea and appetite loss, and those painful mouth sores—but losing her hair had been like losing clumps of herself each time she took a shower.

For me, it was like watching my mother unravel.

Edward says something I can't quite hear. Reluctantly, I slide one of my earphones to the side.

"Sorry, what?"

"What are you listening to?" he asks.

Can't this guy take a hint? "The Cranberries."

His mouth slants into a sly smile as he presses a button on the stereo system, filling the car with the thrashing cadence of "Zombie," the fourth track off the Cranberries' new album.

I eye this stranger curiously. Okay, I think, so his taste in music doesn't completely suck.

Maybe getting to know the other side of my family won't be so terrible.

2

MARIAH

M y stomach does a somersault as we drive past an ornate sign that reads, Red Cliff Vineyards, Est. 1977. The vineyard's name is an obvious play on the family's surname, combined with the fact that they only produce red wines.

If I had any food in my stomach, I might be concerned about throwing up, but I was too nervous to eat this morning. As if meeting my father for the first time wasn't stressful enough, now I get to meet his wife and children.

He makes a turn, and soon we're winding through rambling fields of grapevines.

"I told the cook to have lunch ready for you when we arrive," he says. "Chastity's spent the morning getting your room ready. I'm sure you'll want the afternoon to get settled."

"That's nice of her," I say, trying not to sound as doubtful as I feel. Chastity is Edward's wife, which under normal circumstances, would make her my stepmom. But

I'm not sure the term applies if the woman was married to your dad when he knocked up your mom.

Why Edward is so eager to shove his past indiscretions in his wife's face, I have no clue. Maybe he's looking to clear his conscience, or absolve himself in the eyes of the Lord, or whatever it is people do to torture themselves here in Virginia wine country.

"Here we are," Edward says. "Home sweet home."

My gaze sweeps across the great green lawn and the rows of slender trees that mirror each other up the driveway.

Holy shit, I think, *maybe this really is the most enchanted place on earth.*

"That's not a house," I say. "That's a castle." Or, more accurately, an authentic-looking English country estate. Stone-faced and three-storied. I count at least seven chimneys, and two dozen windows on the front-facing side alone.

Edward chuckles. "Wait till you see the winery."

He points to a building across a section of vineyard on the other side of the road. Sure enough, the winery is almost as large as the residence. The design is much more elaborate, with a broad terrace and stone archways that call to mind the old Italian movies my grandpa loved to watch.

The winery wasn't built until after Edward bought the estate, and this new construction was clearly intended to evoke a Mediterranean feel. The mix of styles is a little tacky, if you ask me, but he didn't, so I keep the thought to myself.

"We kept the old gardens behind the winery," he says. "And the old stables are just beyond that."

"You have horses?" My mother had a horse growing up that she loved more than anything.

"Not anymore," Edward says. "We sold them off just before we built the winery so we could extend the growing operation."

"Oh," I say, trying not to sound too disappointed.

As soon as we pull up in front of the house, a man rushes to open my door. I thank him as I exit the car. He removes my suitcase from the trunk and then hands my bag off to another man, who seems to have appeared from thin air behind me. The first man grabs the car keys from Edward's waiting palm, and soon the Ferrari speeds off to who knows where.

Standing in the curved driveway, I'm overwhelmed by the unmistakable scent of lilacs. I inhale deeply, humming with pleasure, before I recall that it's not the right season for them. I glance around to see what flower might be playing tricks on my senses, but I don't see any blooms. Just evergreen shrubs trimmed into perfect rectangles.

A slim blonde appears on the stone steps leading up to the house like a real-life Stepford Wife. Her red lips and nails stand in stark contrast to the whites of her pants and teeth. Edward ushers me toward her, and I experience the fleeting notion that I'm about to be fed to the lions.

"Mariah Katherine Greyson," he says, "I'd like you to meet my wife, Chastity Luann Radcliff."

"How lovely to meet you, Miss Greyson." She takes my hand in hers. "It's about time we were acquainted."

Knowing full well that this meeting is neither lovely, nor timely, I nevertheless respond, "It's nice to meet you, too, Mrs. Radcliff."

"Christopher," she calls over her shoulder. "Come meet Miss Greyson."

A young man around my age emerges from inside the house. He's tall, like his father—like our father, I remind myself—with dark, assessing eyes and a jaw like an anvil. My mom never mentioned Edward having a son, so Christopher must've come along after she and Grandpa moved off the property.

"Mariah," Edward says, "this is my son, Christopher Edgar Radcliff."

"Hi." I offer him my hand, but he just stares at me, his gaze sharp as a needle.

"Manners, Christopher," Chastity says.

Edward clears his throat. Finally, Christopher shakes my hand, squeezing hard enough to evoke genuine concern for my metacarpals.

"There," Chastity says. "Now that introductions are out of the way, your lunch will be served in the conservatory. However, dinner's going to be a bit later than usual tonight. Lilliana got caught up at school."

Lilliana is Edward and Chastity's daughter. She was still in diapers when her dad bought the estate. Too young to remember my mom, though my mom remembered her as a fussy baby with a perpetually runny nose.

Edward frowns at his wife and checks his very large, very shiny Rolex. "I suppose that'll give us time for a tour of the grounds. Mariah, why don't you head up to your room, unpack, and have some lunch. I'll come find you. We can take a stroll through Isabella's old stomping grounds."

At the sound of my mother's name on her husband's lips, Chastity's eyelid twitches like he's just said the C-word in church. Impressively, her smile remains as pure and uncracked as porcelain.

"What a lovely idea," she says. "Miss Greyson, come with me, I'll show you to the guestroom."

Entering the house is like stepping into a time capsule. Nearly every piece of furniture is a finely polished antique. I follow Chastity up the grand staircase to the second floor and down the hall to my room—sorry, *the guestroom*—where the first thing I notice is the enormous bed, topped with fluffy white pillows and a matching duvet. There's a nice rug, a cute vanity, and a big window overlooking the vineyard.

"This is one of our most comfortable guestrooms," Chastity says. "I'm sure it's the Taj Mahal compared to what you're used to."

What I'm used to might not be an exquisitely preserved mansion, but I didn't exactly grow up poor. My grandpa ended up with a lot of money when he sold this place. He invested most of it, and his investments didn't always pay off, but he set aside plenty for me to go to college. The rest, he spent on a modest house in a quiet neighborhood for the three of us—his daughter, her unborn child, and himself.

I think the main reason I never thought much about my father was because Grandpa made damn sure I knew how much he loved me. It was important to him that Mom and

I were well taken care of, long after the stroke that eventually stole him away.

The house we lived in is currently being held in a trust for me, along with my mom's more-than-generous savings, set to be deposited into my bank account three weeks from now, on my eighteenth birthday.

I resent Chastity's assumption that I'm here to mooch off Edward's wealth or her hospitality. Greysons take care of their own, which is more than I can say for the man who waited seventeen years to meet me.

"It's a very nice room," I say, unzipping my suitcase, which is already waiting for me on the bed.

"If I may," she says, in her sweetest southern-belle drawl. "Can I ask, how bad was it? Your momma's passing?"

For my own self-preservation, I try not to think about the days leading up to my mom's death. We knew it was coming, like dark clouds closing in across the plains, but that didn't make the storm easier to weather.

Witnessing her mind slipping away from her had to have been the worst of it. I was used to her talking to people I couldn't see, but this was different. She was all over the place, murmuring incoherently. Saying things like, "I don't want to go back. They're calling me back..."

"Who's calling you where?" I asked, standing over her hospice bed, dabbing at her dry, cracked lips with a damp washcloth. My eyes stung from crying, and I hadn't left her bedside all day, so my stomach was starting to digest itself.

"I told them I wasn't..." she slurred. "I couldn't...not yet..." She was hopped up on so much morphine, it was hard to understand half of what she was saying, and the bits I caught didn't make sense. "Don't trust him. Don't trust his eyes."

"Whose eyes, Mom?"

Her own gray eyes were staring off into another plane. She went quiet for a while, as her breathing slowed. But in the seconds before she took her final breath, she looked directly at me and rasped, "I'll see you soon."

I'm not sure whether she was talking to me, or if she even knew I was there. But her words gave me goosebumps like cold rain sliding down my back.

My throat tightens at the memory. I start pulling things out of my suitcase and piling them haphazardly onto the bed.

"It was really bad toward the end," is all I can bring myself to say to Chastity.

She nods, like she suspected as much. "Well, however badly your momma suffered, it wasn't enough to make up for what she did to this family. She got what she deserved."

My mouth falls open. Did she really just say that to me?

I stand rooted, mouth gaping, as she paints the smile back onto her face as easily as smoothing on lipstick.

"Come on down when you're ready for lunch," she says.

3

WILLIAM

The girl is still staring at the open door long after Chastity has turned on her designer heels and strode into the hall.

"Bitch," she whispers, as her tears start to fall.

I move around her, studying her from different angles. She's got Radcliff blood in her for sure. I can sense it. But it wasn't until I heard Isabella's name that I took a long, hard look at her.

Could this really be Isabella's daughter? If she is, why can't I sense her power?

I'm standing four feet away from the girl, yet she cannot see me. I was out among the vines when she and Edward pulled up to the house, and at the top of the front steps during her icy introduction to the family.

I follow her into the attached bath where she pulls a wad of toilet paper off the roll and blows her nose, then sits on the closed seat with her head in her hands.

Soft cries deepen into stilted, gut-wrenching sobs.

Watching her fall apart stirs a need inside me that I haven't felt in years: the desire to provide comfort. It's a strange and unfounded feeling, this urge to pull her close. To stroke her face and assure her it'll all be okay.

Must be the hunger talking...

"Mom," she croaks. "I don't think I can do this. I tried to be strong, but I feel so brittle... It was easier to be brave for you because I didn't want you to worry. I know this used to be your home, but I don't feel welcome here. I miss you... Please, give me a sign that you can hear me."

Isabella must've been pregnant when Edward sent her away. I was here the night John and Isabella were unceremoniously evicted from the estate, though I use the term *here* loosely.

Simply put, I am a prisoner on this property. I possess a physical body that hasn't left its cage in almost twenty years.

The only escape I'm afforded is my ability to project myself into the twilight realm—an affectionate name for the dreamlike, superimposed version of the world that serves as a permanent resting place for the dead.

Being perpetually on the verge of starvation has severely limited my psychic abilities. As it stands, I can only venture a few yards beyond the vineyard, and only as a silent observer.

When I'm in my astral form, I cannot interact with the living. The only beings I can converse with, besides my captors, are the spirits who reside here.

Sadly, with only a few exceptions, the ghosts that haunt this estate make for poor company. Perhaps that's an unkind claim to make about my own descendants. But thus is the nature of the twilight realm; it seduces you, lulling you into a stupor, in an effort to soften death's final blow.

Sensing a presence in the other room, I leave the girl to her sorrow and return to find my favorite spirit, Katherine, folding her granddaughter's belongings on the bed.

"Trying to spook her already?" I ask.

"Mariah won't be spooked," Katherine says. "She's one of us."

Katherine was—and still is—a powerful clairvoyant, like her mother before her, going all the way back to the early sixteenth century when my grandson had the misfortune of falling in love with a raven-haired witch. It's how Katherine is able to interact with objects in the physical world—a skill I envy.

Oddly, Mariah doesn't seem to have inherited her forebears' gifts, though she certainly has the look: dark hair, pale skin, and gunmetal-gray eyes framed by thick lashes. She's beautiful and fresh, like a new paint job. But all pure, unpolluted things wind up stained at some point or other.

"Why does Edward want the girl?" I ask. Someone more gracious than me might say it's because he regrets exiling his daughter, but I know the bastard far too well. He never does anything out of the kindness of his corrupt heart.

"He thinks she'll be of use to him."

"Obviously, but how?"

Katherine frowns, then shrugs, which is her way of saying she hasn't had a vision yet.

"Has Isabella seen her?" I ask. Isabella's spirit appeared on the property a few weeks ago, called home by the psychic connection to her family.

"Not yet. John and I agree it's better to wait until she's more lucid." Isabella's spirit made the journey, but she's thoroughly caught up in the miasma of the realm. It could take years before she truly understands where she is and what she's become.

"Does your daughter know who you are?"

A smile graces her bow-shaped lips.

"She does." Having died in childbirth, Katherine never got the chance to hold Isabella in her arms. I imagine having her back here is a bittersweet reunion.

For a ghost, Katherine is exceptionally self-aware. I enjoy her company, as well as her husband, John's. She tolerates mine, and John occasionally visits me in the cellar.

The new blood in the next room has both of them fluttering around the manor like moths.

"You're looking thinner than usual," Katherine says.

"I'll try harder to look healthy for you." One nice thing about astral projection is that I can present myself however I wish, regardless of my physical appearance. It requires a bit more focus, but beats having to walk around looking emaciated and blue-faced from repeated sprayings with colloidal silver. The stuff is like pepper spray for vampires. Get sprayed with it enough times, and it'll start to bioaccumulate, turning your skin blue.

I sense a presence approaching my physical form. Edward, most likely, though he doesn't often visit me so soon after a feeding.

"I'm afraid I must depart," I say. "It appears I'm late for an impromptu bloodletting."

Katherine shakes her head sadly.

I return to my body with a sharp inhale, squinting against the artificial light. Much of the time, I'm shrouded in total darkness. I wouldn't mind it so much if my night vision wasn't compromised from poor nutrition.

"Where do you go, William?" Edward asks, unlocking the door to my silver-coated cage. "Every time I come in here, you look like you're waking up from a dream. But I know your kind do not sleep."

I don't respond. Edward hates being ignored more than anything. I consider it my duty to do everything within my limited power to ruin his fun.

He approaches me without fear because he knows I cannot touch him when I'm chained to the wall. He's rigged up a system of heavy-duty chains attached to silver-coated collar, ankle, and wrist cuffs. With the press of a button, he can loosen the chains and allow me to roam about my enclosure. Or, he can tighten them—like they are now—pinning me firmly against the stone.

Most of the old vampire legends are nothing but fiction. I don't care for garlic, but it doesn't hurt me. The sun won't kill me, though I would need a significant amount of blood and a few days in the dark to recover from a day at the beach.

However, the anecdote about silver being harmful turns out to be true. For a vampire, merely touching it is like placing your hand on a hot stove.

Now, imagine how it would feel to hold your hand there twenty-four seven.

That's been my whole existence for the past eighteen years.

"I hope the boy was to your liking," Edward says, gesturing to the lifeless body of a young man on the floor of my cage. Once a month, Edward and his son will drag an unlucky human down here for me to feed on. He's got it down to a science. One human's worth of blood is enough to enrich every bottle of wine that leaves this place, while keeping me alive and sufficiently weakened.

Edward leaves my cage to fetch an IV needle and a coiled tube from the cabinet where he keeps an array of medical equipment. Back inside, he sets the supplies on a small metal table, next to a bottle of wine and a corkscrew, then takes a seat on the rollaway stool.

"Do you know what tonight is?" he asks.

I maintain my silence.

"Tonight is a monumental occasion." He twists the bottle opener into the cork. "Not only do we have our regularly scheduled family dinner—" He withdraws the cork with a pop. "—but today is also our anniversary."

He means the anniversary of the day he betrayed me.

Before coming to America, I spent a few centuries bouncing around Europe, eastern Asia, and northern Africa with others like me. In the 1930s, I followed my bloodline all the way down and discovered I had descendants living in Virginia, at this very estate. I visited the property, claiming to be a distant cousin, and developed an affection for the place and the people living here. By the mid-seventies, I'd grown tired of wandering around the continent with no place to call home, and decided it was time to secure a permanent residence.

Katherine, one of my descendants, had long-since passed away, leaving her husband, John Greyson, and their daughter, Isabella, to manage the estate. Most of the family money was tied up in the land, and they were struggling to make ends meet.

I got it in my mind to purchase the estate as a home of sorts for myself, as well as the Greysons. I enlisted Edward Radcliff's help in acquiring it, with the intention of making myself known to the family shortly after purchase.

Edward had worked with a vampire I was acquainted with on a similar project, so I thought I could trust him. I gave him my money. He purchased the property.

Then, he made me his blood mule.

Perhaps it was my own doing. Vampire blood has restorative properties for humans. In addition to being incredibly addictive, it can heal them almost instantly. It can make them faster, stronger, and more alert. If they drink enough over a long period of time, it'll slow down the aging process, while clearing up scars and blemishes.

I allowed Edward a taste of my blood when he injured his ankle on the steps to his office. I didn't want an injury getting in the way of the work he was doing for me. However, that one taste was enough to get him hooked.

He takes a long draw off the bottle of wine, then sighs with pleasure.

"God, that's good stuff," he says. He grabs the needle and tubing and begins feeling around the crook of my arm for a vein.

I remember when Chastity first taught him how to do this. Supposedly she used to work for the Red Cross. Now and then, when they can't find a human to feed me, they'll leave a pile of blood bags in the center of my cage. Bagged blood tastes about as good as you'd expect, but it does the trick.

I wince as the needle pierces my skin. Under normal circumstances, I would hardly feel it, but in my current state, every point of contact is a source of pain. He slips the tubing into the mouth of the bottle, sending my blood directly into the wine. I guess the usual drop they add to every bottle isn't going to cut it for tonight's festivities.

"I'd love to stay and chat," he says, "but I'm late to meet my daughter."

"Which one?" I ask through clenched teeth.

His arrogant expression falters. He doesn't know I have the power to watch him and his family whenever I please, and it unsettles him to wonder where I get my information. He corks the bottle and rips the needle from my vein. Blood runs down my forearm to where the silver cuff has burned a wide, raw band into my wrist. It stings.

Edward swirls the bottle, mixing my blood into the wine as he studies me.

"I suppose it's no secret that Isabella and I were involved," he says. As part of the original purchase agreement, Edward offered John and Isabella the option to remain on their family's land. In the guest house, of course. Chastity refused to live under the same roof as *the help*.

Initially, I was perplexed as to why Edward would want them around after he'd assumed full ownership of the estate.

It didn't take long for Edward to make his true desires known.

"You're not exactly subtle," I rasp.

He chuckles. "I imagine you could also hear Chastity shouting about it from all the way down here."

"I hear you shouting," I tell him. "I also hear you fucking. But I haven't heard much from Chastity as of late. Are you neglecting your husbandly duties, Edward?"

He glowers, his gaze flitting to my cock. He hopes to humiliate me by denying me clothes, but when you've been alive as long as I have, you eventually lose all sense of shame—especially where modesty's involved.

In the early days, before I became grotesque, Chastity would sneak down to the cellar to try and get me hard. He caught her blowing me once. Recalling the look on his face when he saw us has gotten me through some difficult times. He still gets jealous whenever I bring it up. However, it's a fleeting satisfaction because Edward is at his most ruthless when provoked.

"We'll try to keep it down tonight," he says, "but no promises." He squeezes the tube with my blood in it, sending deep-red droplets to puddle on the concrete.

The scent of hits my nose and my stomach spasms.

My fangs extend.

He locks my cage and then heads for the exterior door. At the last second, he hits the button to loosen my chains.

I drop to my knees and immediately start lapping at the puddle of blood on the floor. It won't do much to sate me, because it's mine and there's so little of it, but my body doesn't know the difference.

Once my bloodlust sets in, there's no controlling it. I become a slave to my baser instincts, whether it's rage, sex, or hunger. Sometimes all three at once.

"Good dog," Edward says. He switches off the light, bathing me in darkness.

Apparently I was wrong about being entirely shameless.

4

MARIAH

In the time it took for me to have a meltdown in the bathroom, someone has neatly folded and stacked the clothes I dumped out on the bed. I doubt one of the cleaners could've slipped in without me hearing them, much less Chastity in her click-clacking heels.

The back of my neck prickles, a familiar reaction to the realization that although I may be the only one standing here, I'm not alone.

I'd be unsettled if I wasn't so used to the feeling.

"Thanks for folding my stuff," I mumble. "Whoever you are."

I stack my clothing in the dresser, stow my case in the closet, and head downstairs to find food. I get lost twice and have to ask the staff for directions to the conservatory —a sunny, tiled room strewn with potted plants and wicker furniture. A full place setting complete with a covered serving platter rests on the glass table. I lift the lid and find a turkey sandwich and a green salad waiting for me.

To my relief, neither Chastity nor Christopher show themselves in the time it takes me to eat my sandwich. Edward comes to fetch me just as I'm finishing my salad.

We jump in a golf cart and head off on a more detailed drive around the fields, with Edward pointing out the types of grapes they grow. I nod along, half-listening but mostly trying to picture my mom here as a little girl.

"Bet you don't get views like this in the city," Edward says.

"My grandpa used to take us to Assateague to see the wild ponies every summer. We drove through a lot of country along the way."

"Your mother always did love horses." He smiles at me, and I find myself smiling back. As disappointing as my introduction to this side of my family has been, it's nice to be around someone who knew my mom when she was young.

"What was she like back then?" I ask.

"Isabella was the most vivacious person I'd ever met. She was always dancing and singing. She liked to tell fortunes. I had her read my tea leaves every morning just to have an excuse to talk to her. Her knack for predicting things before they happened was extraordinary."

"She had the Greyson gift."

"You're a Greyson." He eyes me curiously. "Do you have the gift?"

I think about the incident with my luggage on the bed.

In general, people reacted one of two ways when they learned that my mom was "gifted." Either they dismissed her as crazy and kept their distance, or they showed up on our doorstep in the middle of the night asking her to summon their dead relatives. Occasionally, the former became the latter, usually after a few drinks. I'm not sure which type Edward is yet, so I decide to keep things vague.

"Not really," I say. "Sometimes I have weird dreams, or see strange shadows, but nothing like my mom. She was the real deal."

He makes the turn for the winery. After a short break in the conversation, he asks, "Did she know she was going to die?"

My throat clenches. "I think she knew a lot sooner than she told me."

"Did knowing it was coming make it easier?"

"I thought it would. But when you know tragedy's inevitable, hope becomes a luxury. It would've been nice to hope, at least for a little while."

He parks in front of the winery. Just as I'm pivoting to climb out, he says, "I never should've let things go as far as they did with your mother. Once you cross a line it just gets easier to cross another, and then another."

I'm not sure what to say to that. "For what it's worth," I tell him, "Mom was a big believer in fate. Whatever's meant to happen will happen, or so she'd say."

He seems happy with this answer. "Well, regardless of how it all came to be, I'm glad you're here now."

We make our way to the stone terrace where couples and groups are seated at high-top tables enjoying glasses of wine and charcuterie. He waves to a black woman wearing a Red Cliff Vineyards apron. She waves back, finishes pouring from the bottle in her hand, and then comes to greet us.

"Mariah, this is Keema Jeffries," Edward says. "She manages the tasting rooms. Keema, allow me to introduce my daughter."

A look of surprise flashes across her face, but she recovers quickly. She asks me where I grew up and if I'm still in school. The usual stuff. It's nice to finally meet someone who doesn't immediately hate me.

Edward and I are about to head inside when Keema says, "Mr. Radcliff, I left a note on your desk. Tony hasn't shown up for his shift in three days."

He frowns. "That's a shame. I liked Tony. If he doesn't come back by Monday, you can post the job in the paper."

The winery's insides are just as elaborate as its outsides. Edward starts by taking me around the kitchens and banquet spaces before leading me into the production area. He shows me the conveyor belts where the grapes are sorted, and the various presses, crushers, and aerators that juice the grapes and oxygenate the wine. We tour the massive fermentation tanks and the storage areas.

Finally, he takes me to the place I've been dying to see: the gardens.

"Isabella spent a lot of time out here," he says. "We kept the overall size the same, and then built this patio to expand the tasting area. People really seem to love it out here."

"I can see why." It's late in the season, and many of the flowers have gone to seed, but plenty of others are in bloom. Walking the garden path is like stepping into a fairytale. I'm convinced there are pixies living in the trees.

Edward gestures for me to take a seat at one of the small, round tables.

"So, what did you think?"

"It's beautiful," I say. "I see why my mother loved it here."

"Maybe in a few weeks, you'll find you love it so much you won't want to leave."

I smile politely. My mom may have grown up here, but it's been almost twenty years since she left. I'm a stranger to this place, no more tied to it than I am to the stranger seated across from me.

"Edward, I appreciate you bringing me out here, but you have to know I'm only here because my mom told me to come. As soon as my inheritance goes through, I'm going home."

He strokes his stubbled chin. "I understand your trepidation, Mariah. You have very little reason to feel tied to this place, or the people who live here. But perhaps instead of looking at this trip as a favor, you could try and see it as an opportunity."

"An opportunity for what?"

"To get to know the other side of yourself, and your family."

"Um, Edward, in case you haven't noticed, your wife and son aren't exactly enthusiastic about hosting me."

"I apologize for the cold welcome. My son needs time to get used to the idea." He checks his watch. "We should get back soon. Lilliana will be arriving shortly. You picked an excellent weekend to come. With my work schedule and the kids' extracurriculars, the whole family only gets to sit down to dinner once a month."

"I didn't exactly choose this weekend," I remind him.

We make it back to the house just as the sun is setting. The lilac aroma is gone, and I'm beginning to wonder if I imagined it altogether. Rather than invite Chastity to bite my head off, I decide to put on something nicer than ripped jeans and a band tee for dinner. I opt instead for a rose-printed, baby-doll style dress and brown chunky sandals.

Everyone's already seated around the dining table when I arrive, including a young woman I haven't met. I figure she must be Lilliana. Unlike her brother, she doesn't glare at me like she wants to slit my throat. She barely acknowledges me, and when she does, it's with the same indifference she grants the steamed carrots on her plate.

Chastity clears her throat as I take my seat in the place that's been set for me, beside Christopher.

"How good of you to finally join us, Miss Greyson," Chastity says. "I thought you'd gotten lost."

"Come now, darling," Edward says. "Mariah's not the reason we're sitting down so late. Lilliana, I trust you had a valid reason for forcing us to postpone our scheduled dinner."

I steal a glance at the young woman across from me. Bathed in the glow from the antique chandeliers, she looks like she could be a model.

Now that the whole family's here, it strikes me just how good-looking they all are.

Edward and Chastity must be in their forties, but neither appears to be going gray or sprouting more than the tiniest of wrinkles. Lilliana looks like she stepped right off the set of *90210*. Her spun-gold waves are darker than her mother's curls, but lighter than Christopher's chestnut locks. Shiny hair, clear complexions, and bright eyes abound. Not a spare pound or a stray hair among them.

Are these people even human?

"I was working on a group project," Lilliana says. "My partner ran late—"

"You know better than to offer me excuses," says Edward. "Lilliana is a sophomore at James Madison University," he says to me. "She's double-majoring in business and finance. Hoping to secure herself a directorial position here at the vineyard. Christopher intends to do the same. Isn't that right, son?"

"Yes, sir," he says.

"We'll see which one of you makes the cut." Edward frees the cork from an open bottle of the vineyard's Pinot and begins pouring. Lilliana's barely a year older than me, and Christopher and I aren't eighteen yet, but Edward pours us full-sized glasses anyway.

"It's tradition," he says with a wink. "Where's the fun in living on a vineyard if you can't enjoy the fruits of your labor?"

I don't live on a vineyard. And I'm willing to bet no one at this table has spent a single afternoon laboring in the fields.

"When in Rome," I say.

Taking his seat at the head of the table, Edward raises his wineglass, and the others raise theirs. I do the same.

"Blood, family, legacy," he says. "These are the foundations of a good life and a great business. Blood is everything. It is where you come from, what you are, and often, an indication of how far you will go."

Chastity scrapes an impatient fingernail against the cream-colored tablecloth. Lilliana frowns at her plate. Christopher listens intently, like a soldier awaiting orders. As for me, I'm just trying to get through the moment with a straight face.

Blood is everything? Is this guy serious?

"Mariah is a member of this family," says Edward. "I hope that we can all do our best to welcome her into the fold. Her lineage is rooted deep within these lands. Her blood is in the soil, the fruit, in the wine itself. I have no doubt that she will bring something very special to this operation." He lifts his glass higher. "To the bonds of family."

"To family," Chastity says flatly.

"To family," Christopher echoes.

Lilliana glares at her brother. "To family."

Four pairs of eyes settle upon me.

I clear my throat. "Right, family."

Edward brings the glass to his lips and drinks deeply. Chastity follows suit. Christopher and Lilliana drink, as well, and although I've never been a big fan of the stuff, I figure I might as well finish off the tour with a tasting.

I don't expect to like the wine as much as I do. It's smooth, but not bland. Bitter yet sweet, with hints of ripe plums, tart cherries, and the tang of copper pennies.

Before I know it, I've downed half my glass.
"Good, yes?" Edward says, smiling at me.
I dab the corners of my mouth and nod.
"Delicious."

5

MARIAH

Mercifully, the rest of dinner goes by without another cryptic speech. The food is decent, the conversation light, though Edward's odd habit of pitting his kids against each other actually has me feeling sorry for them. It's no wonder they started out hating me; he did everything he could to put them on the offensive, short of introducing me as the next challenger for the Red Cliff throne.

Before anyone can suggest a game of Monopoly, I thank Edward and Chastity for dinner and excuse myself to my room for the night. I take a hot shower and crawl into bed to listen to some Nirvana. Halfway through "Come as You Are" I have to switch to The Cure, because thinking about Kurt Cobain has me missing my mom again, at a time when all I want is to forget about my own life and the things I've lost.

In three weeks, I'll be home, I tell myself. The house I grew up in will be mine, and I'll have enough money to live there by myself for a while, as I figure out my next move.

I'm drawn into the shallow depths of a restless sleep by the breathy voice of Robert Smith promising to always love me.

My mind wanders through various dreamscapes like an innertube floating downriver. I'm in a car on the highway going eighty, even though I don't have my license. I'm trying to order spaghetti at a restaurant, but I have no mouth. My server, a large red-haired woman, gets impatient with me and moves on to a different table. I cry red-wine tears that stain the tablecloth.

I'm pulled back to consciousness by the sound of laughter tittering through the window. I open my eyes and realize that I'm no longer in bed. I'm not even in the guestroom. I'm in the conservatory.

Rising from the chair I've somehow found myself in, I take a few tentative steps toward the open French doors leading out to a patio. It's twilight, though I can't say for certain if the sun is setting or rising. The sky is a gradient stretching from cotton-candy pink at the horizon to deep violet up above. I pass through the doorway, and a light breeze ruffles my hair and makes my nipples tighten inside my tee shirt.

I inhale the perfume of lilacs, and watch the horses grazing among the vines. Then I remind myself that it's October, and there aren't any horses on the grounds anymore.

That's how I know I'm still dreaming.

I've been a lucid dreamer since I was little, capable of controlling my consciousness at whim while asleep. It's the one Greyson-like talent I've been blessed with, and it's not even that interesting.

A burst of laughter calls my attention to a couple drinking champagne on the patio. I approach them. They ask if I'm wearing *that* to the party, and it's not until I notice how they're dressed—her in a silk blue wrap dress with ruffles, and him in a fedora and striped jacket—and the way their silhouettes dissolve slightly into the air around them, that I realize they aren't just stand-ins manufactured by my dream engine.

They're ghosts. My mom tried describing them to me, but it's one thing to hear about something and another to actually see it with your own eyes.

Ghosts don't look the way you might expect, all white-sheeted and billowy. Neither do they resemble rotting corpses. They look like shimmery versions of regular people. A little fuzzy around the edges, maybe, but otherwise normal.

The clamor of horn-heavy music playing elsewhere on the estate coaxes me to step barefooted into the grass. I make my way toward the sound. Sure enough, there's a party in full swing in the grand foyer. I peek through the windows at the crowd of ghosts having a grand old time, drinking, laughing, and dancing.

I stay and watch for a while and listen to the band play, until a man in a waistcoat comes up behind me and asks if I have an invitation. I run into the field, glancing over my shoulder to make sure I'm not being chased.

A woman in a white dress watches me from a second-story window. I'm not a hundred percent certain, but I'm pretty sure she's watching me from the room I'm staying in. She's too far away to note the details of her face, but her hair is long, dark, and straight, like mine. I blink and she's gone, and her absence unsettles me and sends me galloping further into the grapevines.

The sky hasn't changed since I awoke into the dreamscape, giving the vineyard a sense of timelessness. Now that I'm away from the house, I make my way down the rows of vines slowly, skimming my fingers over the leaves.

This place isn't so bad without Edward and his awful relatives making me feel unwelcome. It would've been even nicer to have come here with my mother; I could've listened to her tell her own stories.

A crow soars overhead and then drops into a cluster of trees. That's when I spot the man standing with his back to me among the vines.

"Hello," I call out, moving a little closer. He turns his blond head slowly, like he's not sure if he heard me. I call out again, "Hello, sir?"

When our gazes meet, I stop advancing. His eyes are so blue they're almost turquoise. I'm already lost in them, and I just got here. He studies me curiously, like he's never seen a girl in a Blind Melon tee shirt before.

"Did you say something to me?" he asks.

"I said hello."

The man looks around, like he's making sure I'm not actually talking to someone behind him. He's a pretty big guy, fit and brawny. Maybe he's the ghost of a laborer, I think, though his clean shirt and fair skin would suggest he's not one for toiling in the sun. I'd guess him to be somewhere in his mid-thirties. I wonder how long it's been since he passed on, then remind myself he isn't real. This place *looks* like the vineyard, but it's not the vineyard. There's no reason my mind couldn't dream up ghosts just as easily as it cooks up impatient servers.

"How long have you lived here?" I ask. Mom also told me that ghosts sometimes forget they're dead, and when they do, it's best not to remind them. Nine times out of ten, whenever there's an aggressive haunting, it's because a ghost is confused, or hasn't yet come to terms with their situation. This man appears lucid enough, and his silhouette is surprisingly crisp, but I figure it's better to play it safe.

His lip curls slightly. "I've been here much longer than I'd like to be."

"Oh. That sucks." I'm not sure how else to respond.

Two rows of vines separate us, but even that distance and a coating of golden scruff aren't enough to mask the fact that he's handsome. His face is angular without being pointed, his lips full, yet defined. The longer I look at him, the faster my pulse starts to race. Heat floods my face as I force myself to stop gawking at him like some wannabe groupie.

"I'm just visiting my dad," I say, hoping he won't notice the tremor in my voice. The man says nothing. When I allow myself to glance his way again, he's no longer standing in the same spot.

He's right beside me.

I stagger back a few steps.

"How did you do that?" A dumb question, considering ghosts don't have to follow the laws of physics in the real world, let alone the nonexistent rules in my dreams.

I hold my breath as the man reaches out to touch my cheek. Somehow his eyes are even bluer this close up.

"How is this possible?" He strokes the sides of my face.

"Anything's possible in a dream," I say. He shakes his head in disbelief, like *I'm* the ghost in *his* dreams.

"This is why he wants you," he says, and I have no idea what that means.

"Who wants me?"

His gaze lifts over my shoulder, in the direction of the house.

"It's time to wake up, Mariah."

"Why?" *And how does he know my name?*

"You have a visitor." He grasps my shoulders firmly enough to pinch and shakes me.

I'm jolted awake, for real this time.

It takes me a second to recall where I am—in bed, in the guestroom, at Red Cliff—and half a second more to realize that I'm not alone.

A figure stands tall and imposing in the darkness beside my bed. At first, I think it's the man from my dream. But then my eyes adjust, and I see that it's my half-brother, Christopher.

"What do you want?" I ask, my voice hoarse with sleep...and fear.

He tilts his head, illuminating half his face in the moonlight streaming through my curtains, like dipping a cookie into milk. His expression is stern and does painful things to my belly the longer I look at it.

"You're not like I thought you'd be," he says quietly. "My father led us to believe that you were somehow special. That you'd bring something *unique* to the table. But now that I've seen you, it's obvious that you are nothing out of the ordinary. Just another illegitimate brat whose slut mother couldn't keep her legs together."

Anger sets my blood on fire. I sit up and open my mouth to tell him to fuck off, just as his hand shoots out to grab my jaw.

"Never forget that you don't belong here, Mariah."

My heart pounds. His grip dents my skin and makes my jaw ache.

"If you let yourself get comfortable," he says, bringing his face close to mine. "If you even think about overstaying your welcome, I'll have to come back here and remind you where you stand."

He lets go of my face and reaches for something in the vicinity of his waistband. My muscles tense. I brace myself on the mattress, ready to throw him off should he try to climb on top of me.

Seconds tick past. Then I hear the trickle of liquid hitting the bedspread.

I jump out of bed and out of reach of the stream. His piss is acrid smelling. I hold my breath, my stomach winding into tighter and tighter knots.

He's insane, I realize. This whole family is batshit fucking insane.

I close my eyes and wish that I could be anywhere else. But unlike in my dreams, I have no control over what happens. I just have to wait it out.

After emptying an entire pouch of Capri Sun's worth of piss onto the bed, Christopher puts his dick back in his pants.

"You should clean this up before my mom sees it," he says. "Wouldn't want her to think you're a bedwetter, on top of being a whore's daughter."

6

WILLIAM

Mariah vanishes before my eyes, her form dissolving like ashes through my fingers.

I've never known a living human who could physically manifest in the twilight realm.

As a vampire, I can visit this place, but I cannot affect it. Powerful spirits who reside here, like Katherine, can focus their attention to influence objects in the physical world. But the bleeding effect between the realms only goes one way. Isabella was sensitive enough to perceive it, but it takes a very powerful psychic to cross the threshold, even in sleep.

I wave my hand through the air where she recently stood. What Mariah has unwittingly accomplished is so rare as to be unheard of, if not impossible. But she made the jump. I felt her physical presence with my own hands —hands that haven't touched anything solid beyond my cage in years.

I race to the house, reaching Mariah's room just as Christopher is leaving it.

The scent of fear and urine hangs in the air.

Fury boils inside me. What has he done to her? I move to her side and note the wet spot on the bed. The motherfucker has marked the place where she sleeps as a warning.

I fight the urge to chase after him, knowing it'll only lead to frustration that I can't make him pay for his actions.

Mariah collapses in on herself like a folding chair and slides to the floor. She rests her head on her knee, and once again, I'm struck by the desire to pull her close.

Realizing that I could in fact hold her if she were dreaming is like stumbling upon water in the desert. Because if I can hold her, and she can touch me, then perhaps she can touch other things that I cannot.

Like keys, and locks, and silver-coated cuffs.

I had resigned myself to the likelihood that I might spend centuries in the cellar at Red Cliff, first as Edward's captive, then as his children's inheritance, and so on. Opportunities for escape have been so few and far between that I've ceased looking for them.

I couldn't have anticipated a rare psychic like Mariah would be dropped into my lap.

Her abilities must have been dormant, but one taste of my blood has set off a chain reaction inside her. I haven't felt psychic vibrations like the ones she's giving off in centuries.

She lifts her head to rub her eyes, her breathing well on its way to normal. Her cheeks are dry. I'm impressed.

She's going to need that resilience if she wants to survive this place.

But first, I have to find out what else she's capable of. If she can interact with physical objects on her own plane while standing in the twilight realm, then she can, in theory, steal Edward's keys, unlock my cage, and remove my restraints. Once I'm no longer bound, I can slip into the house and feed on the Radcliffs, one by one, to regain my strength.

My gums are already tingling at the thought of sinking my fangs into Edward's carotid artery.

It has to happen soon, while the boy's blood is still fueling me, and I have enough energy to climb out of the cellar. Wait much longer, and I'll be too weak to crawl, let alone stand.

Years ago, I tried reaching out to Isabella, in the days before she and her father left the estate. She thought I was some kind of demon. Mariah will likely assume the same, once she sees what I'm capable of. But by then I'll no longer need her assistance, and she'll be free to get away.

Once I know for certain that she can retrieve Edward's keychain, I'll begin convincing her not to fear the creature in the basement—

"It won't work," Katherine says from behind me. "She's not strong enough to interfere with the physical realm yet. She needs time."

"Unfortunately, I don't have time to spare," I say. Katherine must've finally seen a vision of the future. How...disappointing. I glance at the girl on the floor. "Very well. If she can't recover the keys while she's asleep, I'll just have to persuade her to release me while she's awake."

"You'll kill her," Katherine says.

"Not necessarily."

She shakes her head. I sigh.

"You've seen it happen, then?" I ask.

"I've seen you. Hunched over her lifeless form, her throat shredded." She regards her granddaughter with a look of despair. "She's just a child, William."

"You're all children to me, Katherine." I head for the door. Katherine follows on silent feet.

I sense the aura of her anguish all around us, and it chafes. She knows as well as I do that this needs to happen. If she could fetch the keys herself, she would have freed me years ago, but they're too heavy for her to carry all the way down to the cellar, even for a spirit with her skill and focus.

"If you've seen it," I tell her, "then you know there's no point in trying to stop me."

She slips in front of me at the head of the stairs. "Hasn't my family suffered enough?"

I surge forward. Such a move might normally intimidate a person as small in stature as she is, but Katherine knows I cannot harm her. Not physically, anyway.

"I have suffered enough," I growl.

She meets my gaze with an equally formidable stare of her own. "Are you so determined to become the villain —"

"I am a villain, or have you forgotten?"

"How could I, after seeing what you did to that boy? You nearly ripped him in half in your frenzy to get at his throat."

"And I'll just as soon do the same to your granddaughter."

She finally looks away, and I continue my descent, passing through her on my way to the ground floor.

Katherine and her husband have been kind to me in my captivity. I will mourn the loss of their companionship when the time comes. But if it's between remaining Edward's prisoner and breaking the ephemeral hearts of a few ghosts, I'll shatter those hearts like I long to shatter the cuffs that bind me.

"I am sorry, Katherine. Truly. I won't enjoy killing Mariah, but I won't remain chained to spare her life. Edward needs to pay for what he's done."

She manifests in front of me. "Revenge will not make you whole again, William. Only forgiveness can do that."

I narrow my gaze. "If you think I'll ever forgive that coward for starving me like a dog, then you haven't been paying attention."

I circle Katherine until I'm standing behind her.

"But let me tell you what I will do. I'll tell Edward's daughter whatever lies are necessary to coax her into the dark, dank cellar. I will bribe her, betray her, even seduce her if it pleases me. Anything and everything to convince her to take pity on this poor confined creature. Once I'm free, I will drink from her until my strength has been restored."

Katherine shudders.

"And then," I continue, "after I've had my fill of Edward's daughter, I will kill him, and the rest of his miserable family, before I burn his vineyard to the ground."

7

MARIAH

With my heart rate finally under control, I throw on yesterday's jeans, tuck in my oversized tee, and shove my feet into my sandals. Careful not to let the wet spot touch me, I gather the soiled bedding and sneak downstairs in search of the laundry room.

The clock in the foyer says it's just past four in the morning. Thankfully, the staff don't appear to be up and about. I discover the laundry room tucked behind the butler's pantry and toss my bedding into the wash. I leave a note for the staff claiming I spilled soda on my sheets and then slip out the kitchen door into the early-morning chill.

Dew on the grass makes my feet slippery inside my sandals. I tread out to the patch of vineyard where I ran into the man in my dream. It's dark, and I nearly trip twice. The air is heavy and cold. I could kick myself for forgetting to grab my grandpa's flannel.

Smoothing the gooseflesh from my arms, I glance around to make sure I'm alone. Unlike in my dream, there's no music, no dancing ghosts, no mysterious man reaching out to touch me. Just the sound of crickets chirping, and a few distant stars on the horizon.

I didn't expect the man to be here waiting for me. It's not like he is—or was—a real person.

Even so, I can't recall ever having such a vivid dream about a real-life location. The whole thing felt more like an out-of-body experience.

My mom used to wander around our neighborhood while she slept, snooping in people's windows and backyards. "The Careys finally got a thicker set of curtains," she'd tell me the next morning. Or, "Looks like it's Mrs. Sullivan who isn't cleaning up after her dog."

I would've liked to have woken up with a funny story to tell about my first nighttime walk about, instead of waking up and being pissed on.

What Christopher did to me was nothing short of vile. I don't know whether to be more terrified or disgusted. He didn't exactly hurt me, but the potential was there, and that was the point.

He wanted me to know that things could get worse—a lot worse.

Coming here may have been a mistake, but it's not like I had much choice in the matter. My mom was convinced that this is where I need to be right now. Had she seen what Christopher would do to me? Had she heard the awful things his mother would say?

Mom didn't always tell me everything she saw in her visions. I think she wanted to afford me as much normalcy as possible, even when I begged her for a heads up. What's the point of having a mom who can see the future if she can't help you avoid embarrassment or heartbreak?

When I begged her to tell me if my first high school boyfriend was going to break my heart, she said, "Knowing about awful things before they happen is only helpful if you can prevent them, and we can't prevent them. Things happen the way they're meant to. You can only brace yourself and prepare for what's coming."

"But you could *help* me brace for it," I said.

She just shook her head. "Trust me, sweetheart. It's better not to know."

Of course she was there when I found out he was cheating on me a week later, waiting in the car outside his house with two of my favorite candy bars and a box of tissues.

I'm still on the fence as to whether I agree with her that it's better not to know about things before they happen.

I walk the rows of vines as the sun begins to announce itself on the horizon. Eventually, I'm joined by the growers, a few of whom smile hesitantly as I wish them good morning. I can only imagine what the Radcliffs have said or done to make these people so wary of speaking to me.

As I cross into another section of vineyard, the trees in the distance seem clearer somehow. Crisper. I barely have to squint to see the individual leaves. I find myself noting specific sounds, too, independent from the noise around them. One bluebird's call over another, the rumble of a tractor over the gnashing of a woodchipper.

Something whispers over my right shoulder. A murmur of feelings rather than words, but the meaning is the same: *move.*

I feel the object coming before I hear it, and I duck.

An arrow whooshes past me and embeds itself into the ground.

My heart punches at my sternum as every muscle in my body goes taut.

Again, I sense the whisper like a warning, this time to my left. I roll.

Another arrow strikes the ground.

"What the fuck..." On hands and knees, I scramble to the end of the hedgerow and sit with my back to the trellis. My pulse gallops in my head like horse hooves. I try peering over the vines to see if I can tell where the arrows are coming from, but the foliage is too high.

A third arrow comes down a few inches from my foot.

Yelping, I scuttle down an adjacent row until I reach the edge of the field, then start sprinting along the perimeter toward the house. My lungs burn. My side aches like I'm being stabbed. As I approach the manicured lawn, I see Lilliana standing with her back to me.

I slow to a jog and then stop, panting.

Lilliana grabs an arrow from the quiver at her feet and draws the bowstring back on an expensive-looking bow. She's set up a target a few yards away, in the opposite direction of the vineyard.

She releases the arrow. It hits the bullseye dead-on.

"What the hell?" I say, breathless. "You could've fucking killed me."

She glances over her shoulder at me and shrugs.

"Sorry," she says, not sounding sorry at all.

I rest my hands on my knees. Lilliana aims, draws, and shoots another arrow, landing it in almost the exact same spot as the first.

"How'd you know to duck the first time?" she asks.

I don't know how I knew the arrow was coming, but I'm not about to sit down and discuss the possibilities with her over breakfast.

With my heart no longer working to hammer its way out of my chest, I march across the lawn and into the house in search of Edward.

I find him in his office on the third floor.

"I think Lilliana just tried to kill me," I tell him.

"She's the top archer on her team, two years running." He studies the papers on his desk. "Trust me, if she wanted you dead, you wouldn't be standing."

"So, I'm target practice, then."

He glances up from his work and lowers his glasses. "How'd you sleep?"

"Like a baby with colic who wants to go home."

"But you just got here." He beckons me to stand with him at the antique cabinet by his desk. "Come, take a look at this."

"You're not listening to me," I say, joining him.

"I am listening. I just think you should see this first."

A crossbow hangs on the wall beside the cabinet. I suppress a groan. *Like father, like daughter.*

The cabinet itself is made of a dark, sturdy hardwood, but the doors are mostly glass. An array of heirloom items populate the shelves. Crystal goblets, a small hand-carved chest, porcelain figurines, and some framed black-and-white photos.

The fury I walked in with begins to subside as I realize what I'm looking at: my family's lost treasures. I haven't seen old photos in any of the other parts of the house, so I'm surprised, and admittedly excited, to find these.

"These were all taken here?" I ask.

"I believe so. I told Chastity she could redecorate every room in the house except this one. I like to maintain a bit of vintage charm."

There are photos spanning all the way back to the early twentieth century, judging by the clothes and the dates written on some of the photos. I pause on a faded photo of four women in white dresses sitting in what's now the living room, and another featuring a group of dusty men working in the fields.

I smile at a more recent picture of Edward shaking hands with my grandpa.

"When was this one taken?" I ask, pointing.

"That was taken the day the estate sale went through."

And that explains why my grandpa looks so happy; he'd just become a very rich man. However, as excited as my grandpa must've been about the money, I know he had reservations about selling my grandmother's childhood home. He would've preferred to have held onto it forever, if possible.

"Grandpa told me you approached him about buying the property," I say. "How'd you find out about this place?"

"A gentleman came to me and asked if I would assist him in acquiring the property. He provided the funds, with the understanding that I would develop the estate into a profitable business venture."

"Some random guy just gave you a boatload of money to open a winery?"

"He did. Though, I've assumed full ownership over the years."

"Who was he?"

"That's the thing about silent partners," Edward says. "They prefer to remain anonymous."

"Fine. Keep your wine-soaked secrets." I bring my face closer to the glass so I can study a particularly nice set of hand-carved smoking pipes.

"I'm hoping to make them your secrets someday," he says. "When you join the family business."

I suddenly remember why I stormed all the way up here.

Straightening, I turn from the cabinet to face him.

"Edward, I can tell you're trying to make me feel at home, but I don't feel welcome here. And more than that, I don't feel safe."

He sighs. "I am sorry about Lilliana. She can be petulant."

"It's not just Lilliana. It's Chastity and Christopher—"

"What did my son do?" His gaze narrows. I shift uncomfortably. "Did something happen that I need to know about?"

I want to crawl out of my skin just thinking about what Christopher did to me. "He came into my room last night and warned me not to get comfortable. Which he then punctuated by pissing all over my bed."

Edward runs a hand over his face. "Please allow me to apologize on behalf of my children. They are afraid of losing my favor."

"It's not a competition."

"Life is a competition, Mariah."

"But you're making it worse by pitting us all against each other." I fold my arms across my chest. "Look, I just think it would be better if I went home."

"No, Mariah." He takes my hand. "That would make me very unhappy. Now, I am so, so sorry. What Christopher did was revolting. I will talk to him, and Lilliana."

"And Chastity?"

"Yes, and Chastity. That is a promise."

"I'm not sure it'll be enough." I free my hand from his grasp and turn back toward the cabinet. My gaze catches on a group photo I hadn't noticed before, one with the year 1937 scrawled in black ink at the top righthand corner.

A familiar stare reaches out and grabs me from almost sixty years in the past.

It's the man from my dream, looking exactly the same as he did last night, but with different clothes.

"See someone you recognize?" Edward asks.

"No," I say quickly. I don't want to have to explain my dream man to Edward. It feels too personal, and I'm not even sure what to make of it yet.

My palms start to sweat. I had never seen this man before, so I know I didn't conjure him from memory. But if he was here in 1937, then that means his ghost is real, which then begs the question, are the other ghosts real, too? Why am I suddenly seeing ghosts in my dreams?

And, most importantly, how was the man able to touch me?

"Are these the only old photos you have, or are there more?" I ask.

"I'm afraid Chastity threw most of them out during the renovation," he says. "But she may have packed a few albums away."

"I think I'd like to see those."

"I'd like for you to see them, too." He takes my hand again. "You're not a prisoner, Mariah. If you really want to leave, I'll drive you to the airport myself. But if I can get Christopher to assure me that he is *very* sorry for his actions, will you consider staying a while longer?"

I steal another glance at the old group photo. If the man from my dream really is a ghost, then the only chance I'll have to talk to him again is if I stay one more night.

"Fine," I say. "But if things don't get better, I'm out of here."

8

WILLIAM

E dward whirls the silver keychain around his finger, glaring back and forth between his disobedient children. He's brought them down to the cellar to give them a talking to. It's a speech he could easily perform in his office but having a bloodthirsty vampire at his back certainly helps punctuate his points of contention.

"I thought I'd made myself clear before Mariah's arrival," Edward says. "But apparently you both need everything spelled out for you."

Lilliana sighs, arms folded, outwardly aloof. It's an art she's perfected over the years, masking her emotions with indifference. But her insides tell a different story. Her heart is pounding. She hates being down here, the same way a fast-food junkie would squirm if they had to watch a cow having its throat cut.

Christopher stands motionless like a toy soldier with swampy armpits. He knows he's in for it.

Frankly, these family dramas bore me. It's the middle of the day, and I want them to leave so I can watch Mariah from the twilight realm until she falls asleep. But I prefer not to leave my body unattended around this crowd, even if I can't control what they do to me.

Tonight, I will test Mariah to see if she's capable of retrieving Edward's keys while in her astral form. Katherine claims she's not strong enough, but I'll discern that for myself. At the very least, I can begin earning her trust.

"Whether I choose to disclose certain aspects of my plans to one or both of you is at my discretion," Edward says. "As my children, it is your duty to do as I say, and to trust that I have the situation under control." He looks to his daughter. "What do you have to say for yourself, Lilliana?"

"I wanted to see if she'd predict the arrow's trajectory," she says.

"And. Did she?"

"Maybe. She knew exactly when to duck and roll, so that's something."

Edward rubs his chin. "I cannot condone your acting out against her without my consent. But I appreciate your motivations."

Lilliana's mouth slants into the closest shape it will ever come to resembling a smile.

"Two thousand dollars off this month's allowance," Edward says.

Christopher scoffs. "That's all she gets for trying to kill the little bitch?"

Lilliana smirks. Poor Christopher. Always playing runner-up to Edward's firstborn. His favorite. His Venus fly trap. When Lilliana was fourteen, Edward made her strip in front of a full-length mirror and proceeded to map every spot on her body that needed improvement. She repeated the process herself every night from that point forward, vowing to eradicate every imperfection in an effort to become Daddy's perfect weapon.

"As for you," Edward says, turning to his son. "Pissing all over Mariah's bed is in direct violation of the orders I gave you."

"Disgusting," Lilliana murmurs.

Christopher seethes. "I was sending her a message."

"And what message was that?" Edward snaps. "That she should leave as quickly as possible? How does that serve us?"

The boy purses his lips. Edward moves closer, getting in his son's face.

"You are a spoiled, envious child who would rather throw a tantrum than consider the bigger picture."

Edward unlocks the door to my cage.

"Get in," he says to Christopher.

Lilliana's gaze widens. Christopher's throat contracts as he swallows. He's tall enough and likely strong enough to give his father a run for his money. But what keeps him from shoving the older man into my cage and closing the door is the impact of seventeen years of abuse and manipulation.

This is hardly the first time Edward has brought the two of them down here, though it's the first time he's forcing one of them to get close to me. Normally, he makes them stand outside the cage and watch in horror as I sink my teeth into a disposable member of their staff.

Christopher shuffles through the doorway, his heartbeat hammering in in his chest. I can smell his fear, as well as his blood, and it makes my stomach muscles tighten.

"If I loosen those chains," Edward says, "what do you think will happen?"

"He'll kill me," Christopher says quietly.

"Kill is a pretty word for what that creature will do to you." Edward presses a button on the control panel, loosening my chains. I don't want to help him prove his point to his son, but my hunger is like a force unto itself that can be neither controlled nor contained.

My fangs extend, nicking my lower gums. He smells like everything I want for supper.

I hurl myself toward Christopher. The boy screams. The chains aren't fully loosened, so I can't quite reach him.

"Do you trust that I have our family's best interest at heart?" Edward asks.

"Yes, sir," Christopher shouts, trembling.

"That's a lie," Edward says. "Because if you did, you wouldn't be questioning my choices or trying to speed up my process."

My chains groan as I throw my full weight into them. Christopher's knuckles shine white as he grips the bars.

A familiar scent hits my nostrils as urine pools on the floor at his feet.

"If Mariah possesses even a fraction of her mother's abilities," Edward says, "her blood could be a gamechanger. Imagine how much money we'd stand to make if we were able to see into the future. If we could predict the market before investing."

"You want us to drink human blood?" Christopher asks.

Lilliana rolls her eyes. "Obviously, we'd have this one turn her first, idiot."

Edward smiles proudly at his daughter. There it is, I realize. Edward's petty, human reason for reconnecting with Mariah. Money. Power. The chance to acquire more wealth than he and his wretched family know what to do with.

The assumption that I could simply turn Mariah is ludicrous, considering my current state. It would require me to only drink a portion of her blood. The enzymes in my saliva would do the rest as her organ systems start to fail. However, even if I possessed the wherewithal to partially drain her, the process only works a fraction of the time.

Edward pushes a button on the panel, and I'm snapped back against the stone wall. Christopher slides down the bars of the cage into his own piss puddle. His father unlocks the door and eases it open, blocking the way out.

"Disobey me again," he says, "and I'll leave you in here overnight."

9

WILLIAM

Watching Edward's children deliver their half-assed apologies is as entertaining as it is cringe-inducing. Lilliana's efforts are about as boring and black-and-white as it gets, while Christopher's are much more colorful.

"I am mortified by and deeply ashamed of my thoughtless actions last night," he says. "Please allow me to apologize for my disgusting behavior. It was unacceptable and entirely unwarranted. I vow to be a better, more considerate version of myself going forward."

I can tell from Mariah's body language that she isn't buying a word of it. Clever girl. She spent most of the day in her room, listening to music on her portable device. I hoped she might take a nap, but she was too anxious.

She shifts uncomfortably in her seat and says, "Thank you, Christopher. I appreciate your attempt at an apology."

I wait for Mariah in the twilight realm after she goes to bed, hoping she'll come look for me in the vineyard. I don't want to come off as too eager to see her again.

The craftiest predators know to let their prey come to them.

Her footfalls sound in the grass about a quarter mile from where I lie between two vine rows. It's odd how differently my vampiric abilities behave on this plane. My sense of hearing is just as sharp, but my sense of smell is so dulled it might as well be nonexistent. It's for the best, really. Being able to smell Mariah's blood, but not access it, would be torture even if I wasn't starving. As far as physical restrictions go, I can pass through doors, but not the ground, and I can walk on floorboards, but my hand glides right through other physical objects like shelves and tables.

I pretend to be lost in thought as Mariah approaches, dressed in another one of her extra-long tee shirts.

"Hello again," she says, smiling.

"Hello to you."

She drops down beside me and crosses her legs. "What, you're not going to grab my face this time?"

"I would hardly say that I *grabbed* your face the last time we met," I say. Her bare legs glow in the low light, pale and smooth. I resist the urge to run my hands all over them, just to see if it's possible. "As for whether it'll happen again. Maybe later. If you're lucky."

She chuckles at this. I turn my gaze toward the sky and listen to her heartbeat. She fidgets with a blade of grass.

"I know what you are," she says.

I tense. "Do you?"

"You're a ghost. I saw an old picture of you in Edward's office. The date said 1937."

I roll onto my side to look at her. "Couldn't have been me, sweet pea. I was already dead."

"I'm sure it was you." She rips off a fat blade of grass and rolls it into a ball that stains her fingers. "What's your name?"

"William," I say. "But you can call me Will."

"Nice to meet you, Will. What's your last name?"

"Why do you want to know?"

She shrugs. "Just curious."

"You planning to look me up on your family tree tomorrow?"

"Maybe." She grins.

"Clever trick," I say. "What's a clever girl like you doing up so late on a school night?"

"I've already graduated," she says. "Now don't change the subject. What's your full name?"

I suppose it can't hurt her to know. It's not like she'd be able to confirm the details without consulting a historian. "William Ashton Durant."

She squints. It's kind of adorable. "I don't recall my grandpa mentioning any Durants in our family."

"There haven't been any for quite some time."

"How much time?"

I make a show of tallying the centuries off on my fingers. "Only about...five hundred years or so."

"You're full of shit," she says, tossing a blade of crumpled grass at me.

I pretend to be offended.

"If you're that old," she says, "how is there a photo of you in the house? Also, this estate was built way later than that. How can you be haunting a place you've never lived in?"

"Some ghosts haunt objects. Others haunt people."

"What do you haunt?"

"Your dreams, obviously."

She shakes her head. "Is there, like, a vase somewhere in the house that you belong to?"

"Do I look like a genie to you?"

"I don't know. I've never seen one. Technically, I've never seen a ghost either."

"I'm not a ghost."

"But you just said you were dead."

"Dead doesn't necessarily equal ghost."

She eyes me like I must have a few screws loose.

"Well," she says, "if you're not a ghost, then you're a figment of my imagination."

The possibility that I might just be a very elaborate fever dream seems to disappoint her greatly.

I brace for the shock of physical contact and reach for her hand. She's warm to the touch. I want to press her palm to my face, or smooth it under my shirt. Disperse her heat all over me so I can recall what it feels like to have a body that does more than ache.

"Perhaps you're a figment of mine," I say.

"I doubt that." She frowns. "But hey, if I am, do me a solid and imagine me literally anywhere else."

"Where would you like me to imagine you?"

"Home." She sighs, her gaze wistful.

"And where is home for you?"

"The house I grew up in," she says. "It's in Baltimore."

"That might be a bit further than my range will allow. Why not just go there yourself?"

She cradles her jaw in her hand. "Before my mom died, she told me I needed to come here. She didn't tell me why. But now, something's happening to me. I don't understand it, but I know it has to do with this place. I couldn't see ghosts before, and now I can. In my dreams, at least. I feel like part of me is waking up after a long sleep."

The dormant psychic parts of her are indeed waking up, but it's not because of this place. It's because of my blood. Whether she'd be horrified to know the truth or see my pain as a means to an end, like her siblings do, remains to be determined.

"I keep thinking, if I can see ghosts in my dreams, maybe I can see my mom's ghost someday. I'm afraid if I go home too soon, before I figure out what's happening to me, I'll lose the ability to see them altogether."

She allows herself a moment of sadness before springing to her feet and offering me both her hands.

"Well," she says, "if you're just a figment of my imagination, then I know what I want to do with you."

A trill of arousal—a sensation I haven't felt in years—zips through my bloodstream. I rise and take her hands.

"What's that?" I ask.

"Dance with me," Mariah says, already swaying to the music in her head. I haven't danced in decades, but I remember the moves well enough.

"All right," I say. "Let's go."

I pull her toward the house where the resident ghosts are always celebrating, convinced they're attending a party that never seems to end. She hesitates as we approach the doorway.

"Wait, we can't go inside—"

The doorman gives Mariah and me a onceover. She tries to hide behind me, pulling the hem of her shirt lower.

"Sir," he says to me, "Do you have an invitation?"

"We're with the band," I say, and he opens the door for us.

"It doesn't matter what you say to him," I yell over the swing-style music. "He always lets you in."

Mariah is still laughing as I draw her onto the dance floor. I pull her toward me and then spin her around. She laughs, and I can't get enough of the sound, or this feeling. The lightness in my feet and in my body. It's infectious.

I'd forgotten what it felt like to just have...*fun*.

The band slides into a slow song. Mariah eyes me nervously, like a girl at her first high school dance. She's practically young enough to fit the description.

Again, I'm struck by the urge to pull her close and assuage her. So, that's exactly what I do, taking her hand and resting my own on the small of her back. She leans her head on my shoulder. It's a damn good thing I can't smell her, otherwise my fangs would be buried in her throat.

Instead of savoring her taste, I revel in her solidity, as we sway to the gentle rhythm of the slow song. Her heart beats between us like a bird's wings. I'm caught off guard by how remarkable it feels to simply hold her. She's the only person I can touch within this realm, and it's taking all of my patience and control not to overwhelm her with my desire to make contact.

Mariah clasps her hands behind my neck, pressing her body to mine. My control wavers as my awareness narrows to the places where our forms touch. My chest. Her breasts. Our arms and hands. I slide my palms to her hips and, without thinking, angle my face into the curve of her neck.

My fangs extend. If I were to bite her now, she would feel it, but no blood would flow from the wound. What's odd is that I don't wish to bite her out of hunger. For a vampire, feeding can be an intensely intimate act when it's not a matter of life-or-death.

Under different circumstances, she might offer her blood to me freely. But that's not the world we live in.

The song ends, and I suddenly recall why we're here and what I need from her.

She pulls away, tucking a lock of hair behind her ear, red-cheeked and flustered. The understanding that she's aroused sends a rush of awareness to body parts that haven't experienced pleasure in far too long.

"I'd like to see this old photo of me you were talking about," I say.

She nods, no doubt grateful for the distraction. "It's upstairs."

What a fortunate coincidence that the mysterious photograph she wants to show me would be housed in the same cabinet as the keys to my cage. I've stood in this exact spot countless times, watching helplessly as

Edward placed the keys in a small, hand-carved chest on the middle shelf of the cabinet.

"I don't know," I tell her, pretending to look carefully at the photograph of myself surrounded by relatives that are far closer relations to her than they were to me at the time. "He doesn't look that much like me."

"He looks exactly like you," she says emphatically.

"The eyes aren't right. Maybe if you brought it closer."

She reaches out to grasp the handle on the cabinet, and her fingers glide right through. She gasps.

"That was weird," she says.

"Try picking up the photo itself."

Mariah gives me a strange look. She tries again, and again, but her fingers pass straight through the cabinet, as well as the photo.

"I can't," she says.

"One more time," I tell her. "Concentrate."

"I don't want to. It feels weird."

Prickling with frustration, I force myself to take a step back.

So, Katherine was right. Mariah can manipulate spectral objects within the twilight realm, but not objects that only exist on the physical plane. Perhaps that is a skill she could develop, given time and practice.

Sadly, time is something she now has very little of.

"I'm sorry," she says. "I don't know why I'm sorry, but you seem disappointed that I couldn't grab the picture."

I curve my mouth into some semblance of a smile.

"Don't worry about it." I hold out my hand to her. "Come here, Mariah."

After a moment's hesitation, she gives me her hand. I kiss the back of her palm.

In a way, it will be showing her mercy to kill her, rather than giving Edward the chance to turn her into his blood slave. Still, it's a damn shame. She's so refreshingly *alive*.

I'd truly hoped that Katherine was wrong about the extent of Mariah's abilities, the same way I occasionally long for the taste of chocolate or the oblivion of sleep. It's what remains of the human in me. The antiquated, long-dead parts that are convinced the world will be a duller, more barren place without Mariah in it. As though she were the color yellow, and if I were to take her life, I'd be stealing that color from the sunset.

In another place and time, I might have enjoyed her company once she'd had a chance to grow up and into herself. She's younger than my usual preference when it comes to women, but a starving man doesn't have the luxury of waiting for fruit to ripen.

"This is great, though," she says. "Now that I know you're a ghost, I can go home and see my mother. Her spirit's probably there waiting for me."

Her words snap me out of my bout of premature mourning. I've been keeping tabs on Isabella and guiding Mariah away from places she could potentially stumble across her mother. If Isabella were to see Mariah and I together, she might warn her daughter about my intentions just as we're beginning to get closer.

But if Mariah believes Isabella's spirit is in Maryland, there'll be nothing holding her to this place.

"Isabella's not back there," I say.

"You don't know that for sure."

"Yes, I do."

"How?"

"Because she's here." Telling her this is a risk I'll have to take. I can still keep them apart while Mariah's asleep. I'll just have to hope her powers don't develop so quickly that she's suddenly able to see Isabella while awake.

Mariah's brow creases. "Why didn't you tell me—"

We both turn at the sound of Chastity's heels clicking and clacking up the staircase.

"Will," Mariah says, "why didn't you tell me my mom was here?"

"Miss Greyson!" Chastity's knocks ring out like thunder.

"I didn't tell you because...she might not be well enough to see you."

Agony contorts her features. "She's *still* sick?"

"Not like that." I cup her face. I have to convince her to stay before she wakes up. "Death is a transition. She's still acclimating. I'll help you look for her, I promise," I say, when what I really mean is, I'll guide you around the property making damn sure the two of you never cross paths.

Mariah smiles appreciatively before dissolving through my fingers.

And for the first time since I watched her arrive on the estate, I feel like a true villain.

10

MARIAH

My mom is here.

I open my eyes just as Chastity yanks the pillow out from under my head.

"Get up," she says. "Edward wants to see you at the winery, and he insisted I make sure you eat breakfast."

"What time is it?" I sit upright, rubbing the sleep from my eyes.

"It's almost nine. Christopher's already left for school. I won't have you lazing around my house all morning."

I convince her to let me get dressed in peace and promise to meet her in the kitchen. After a quick shower, I pull on a pair of leggings and slip my grandpa's flannel over mom's old Aerosmith tee.

Chastity's already seated at the breakfast table, sipping something from a champagne flute that smells very alcoholic. I take a seat at the place setting across from her, in front of a tall drinking glass containing a thick, red liquid.

"It's vegetable juice cocktail," Chastity says. "Drink up. It's good for you."

"Can I just have toast?" I ask.

"If you drink your juice first."

I take a tentative sip of the intimidating mystery beverage. It's not bad. Kind of sweet, and a little metallic. I drink a few gulps before I need to take a break.

Chastity watches me like she's waiting for the poison to kick in.

"Um," I say, "do you happen to have any old photo albums or loose photographs lying around? Specifically, ones that were here when you guys moved in."

"I doubt it. But I could tell the maid to check in storage. If you insist."

"Please," I say.

"Fine. Now, finish your juice. Edward's expecting you."

"What about the toast?"

Her jaw twitches. "I'll have the cook to make it to-go."

I politely refuse a ride to the winery, opting instead to munch my toast on the walk over. It's a nice morning, sunny and warm. I'm still reeling from my conversation with Will last night. If what he said is true, and my mom's ghost is here, then I need to find her.

Edward's assistant, a short, red-haired woman with glasses, meets me on the terrace. I follow her up to his office. He's on the phone when I enter. He makes the one-minute sign with his finger, then points to the empty chair in front of his desk. I sit.

"I'll call next week to confirm," he says and then hangs up. "Good morning, Mariah. I trust Chastity made sure you had a decent breakfast."

"She certainly did."

"How are you feeling?"

"Fine," I say. He continues to stare like he expects a more detailed answer. "What did you want to talk to me about?"

He clasps his hands on the desk blotter. "One of our tasting-room assistants appears to have left us permanently. These things happen, people come and go. However, that means there's now a job opening assisting the sommeliers who host our winery tours. I'd like you to consider it."

"Is that even legal? I'm not eighteen yet."

He bats away my concern. "What we don't tell Uncle Sam won't hurt him. Besides, I think you'd be good at it. You have a beautiful smile, a friendly demeanor. I know it's not the most glamorous position, but there's always room for growth. And selfishly, I'm hoping it'll make you feel more invested in this place."

If he'd asked me this question yesterday, I would've respectfully said no. But if what Will says about my mom is true, then I need to start looking for her. Unfortunately, I can only do that when I'm asleep.

In the meantime, I guess I have nothing better to do with my days.

"Sure," I tell him. "I'll take it."

"Excellent." He seems surprised by how easily I agreed to the whole thing. "Keema knows you're my first choice so she hasn't posted the position. You can start today."

I spend the majority of my first day working the tasting rooms, collecting dirty wineglasses, and scraping crusted cheese off of wooden boards. At the end of my shift, Keema hands me a packet of information about each wine and tells me to memorize it.

Before I can blink, a week has passed, and I can confidently recite the differences between a Cabernet and a Merlot.

Working at the winery isn't as boring as I thought it would be. Chastity almost never deigns to come out here, and Edward pays me in cash, so he doesn't have to worry about the fact that I'm underaged. There's always plenty of extra cheese and prosciutto to go around and getting to meet new people every day is a nice distraction. Keema's a really great boss, too. She's hardworking, but not a hard ass. And it's nice to have someone friendly to talk to during work hours.

In my dreams, Will and I explore the property, and he helps me look for my mother.

So far, we've found no sign of her.

After the first couple of nights, I began to worry Will might be mistaken about her presence here. Then I wondered if he was lying about it altogether.

"Are you just telling me she's here so I won't go home?" I asked him one night after we'd searched the winery a third time.

He eyed me with a curious expression. "Now why would I do that?"

I didn't want to say what I was thinking. That maybe he wants me around because he's lonely, or because he likes me as more than a friend. That maybe these nights we've been spending together, lounging in the grass, dancing chest to chest, circling the grounds a hundred times, have inspired more than a fondness for each other.

I'd have to be blind not to see the way he looks at me, like I'm some kind of marvel. And he'd have to be oblivious not to notice the way my breathing changes whenever he touches me. I love the way he touches me, like the simple act of our skin making contact is a miracle.

For the first time in over a year, I feel like I've stumbled upon a small, fragile sliver of hope. I have a day job I don't hate on the most beautiful property I've ever stayed on, and I look forward to seeing Will every night.

On my tenth night at the estate, he took me to see the horses.

At first, they were skittish. Only one of them came over to investigate, a gorgeous brown boy with a black mane. Will whispered to him and stroked his flank. I asked how he was able to touch them, when he couldn't touch anything else—besides me. He said animals are grounded spirits, part of the land in intrinsic ways that people are not.

After a few minutes of trust building, the brown horse let Will climb onto his back.

The sight of Will straddling a horse made me want to rub my thighs together. It was like watching an old painting come to life. A soldier riding into battle, or a knight on his trusty steed. His body was made for combat.

He trotted the horse over to me and then pulled me up to sit between his thighs. I prayed he was too distracted to hear my gasp as his arm went around my middle.

"Hold onto his mane," he said.

We rode from one side of the vineyard to the other and back again, the horse's rhythm doing wonderful things to the sensitive parts between my legs. I imagined Will's hands slipping under my shirt to cup my breasts. The fantasy alone was almost enough to make me come right there on the horse, with Will's chest at my back. His arm tightened around my waist, and I swear I felt the whisper of tiny pinpricks scraping my bare shoulder where my oversized shirt had slipped.

When it began to rain, Will climbed off the horse first and then helped me to the ground. My body felt so warm, I expected to see steam rising from it. Will's eyes glowed brightly, bordered by rain-soaked lashes. He looked beautiful with droplets streaming down his face.

I wanted to kiss him so badly.

His hands remained braced around my ribcage, and I longed to know how they would feel under my wet clothes. The first time we slow danced, it was like we were striking flint against steel. Being that close to him, feeling the sturdiness of his body, ignited a spark that started a fire inside me that hasn't stopped burning.

I dated a little in high school, but I've never had sex. For the longest time, it's just been me and my own fingers for company.

These days, I can't fall into bed without immediately reaching for my clit. And when I do, it's Will's face, his body, his mouth that I picture. I want to strip him down and pour myself all over him. But as fascinated by me as he seems, I can't assume he wants me with the same intensity.

I've given him every opportunity to kiss me, but he hasn't made a move. Instead of pulling me closer, he lets go, reaching for my hand as we set off in search of my mother's ghost or move on to some other family-friendly activity.

Sometimes we sit by the fire in the library and read. We talk about books and read passages from our favorites. He asks about my life back in Baltimore, and I listen as he tells me stories about fighting alongside King Henry V in the Hundred Years' War.

Will insists he's not a ghost, but what else could he be? Either he really has been dead for five hundred years, and his spirit somehow found its way to Red Cliff, or he died sixty years ago and dreamed up a history for himself that he can't escape from.

Either way, it's safe to say he's probably too old for me. But he doesn't look or act old, and most importantly, he doesn't *feel* old. He feels constrained. Like he's not operating at his full strength. He reminds me of my mom when she started losing weight and napping more than usual, but she could still go about her day. Will doesn't *look* sick. But looks can be deceiving.

As for me, I feel healthier every day.

Ever since I got here, I've had more energy than I know what to do with. Not to mention those little warnings, the whispers that tell me when I'm about to spill or drop things. I've managed to catch falling wineglasses at work because a little voice in my head told me they were about to tip over.

But the biggest and most recent development has to be the ghosts I've seen in the daytime.

I saw the first one outside my window yesterday morning. He looked like a younger version of my grandpa, standing in the grass, smiling up at me. I blinked and he vanished, leaving behind the scent of lilacs I've come to associate with dreaming.

Next, came the horses. I was reading in the conservatory on my afternoon off and noticed them through the French doors, grazing among the vine rows. The growers worked through and around them. I had to pinch myself to make sure I hadn't drifted off in the middle of a boring scene.

This is how it must've been for my mother, never knowing who or what she'd see when she walked into a room. She called it the bleeding effect, the leaching of the spirit realm into our own. After seventeen years of being blind to it all, why am I suddenly conscious of the bleed-through?

I catch sight of another ghost just as I'm leaving for work the next morning.

It's been a while since I've seen the woman in the white dress in my dreams, and having never gotten a good look at her face, I'm not immediately certain it's her. She stands on the second-floor landing, gazing down at me with sadness in her eyes. She looks familiar, like a distant relation of mine. Though how far back, I'm not sure.

I apologize to Keema for running late. She tells me not to worry about it. I tie my apron on and gather the supplies I'll need for the first round of tastings into my wooden basket, then head out to the garden patio where I'll be assisting the sommelier.

I'm in the process of laying out Red Cliff napkins and coasters when I hear her singing.

My breath catches. I stop and listen to my mother's favorite song of all time. "Landslide," by Fleetwood Mac. She sang it to me when I was little, and continued singing it as I got older, whenever I was sad or sick or heartbroken.

Slowly, I turn from the table toward the garden path.

My mother sits on the stone lip of a raised bed, looking healthier than I've seen her in a long time. Her hair is loose and wild, and there's color in her cheeks. She spins a hibiscus flower between her fingers, singing to it like she used to sing to me.

I clap my hand over my mouth to muffle a sob.

Will wasn't lying. She really is here.

I'm dying to run to her, to throw my arms around her, but I don't want to startle or cause her to disappear. She might not know who I am. *Please, God, let her remember me...*

Cautiously, I make my way over to her.

"Mom?" I say softly.

She glances up. For a second, I'm afraid she doesn't recognize me, and my heart cracks like ice over a pond. Then she smiles.

"Hi, baby." She has a dreamy glint in her eye, but she's clearly happy to see me.

"What are you doing here?" I ask.

"I'm having tea with your grandmother. She should be here any minute."

My grandmother died a long time ago, but my grandpa spoke about her with such vigor and affection that I feel like I really knew her. The thought of my mom getting to meet her own mother makes my heart ache in the best of ways.

More than anything, I wish I could throw my arms around my mother. But I don't want to surprise her if she expects to be able to hold me, and then our hands pass straight through each other.

"How are you feeling?" I ask.

"I'm feeling great, sweetheart. How are you?" She studies me for a moment. "You look strong."

I don't feel strong. I feel like I'm about to shatter into a thousand pieces. Reminding myself to breathe, I fight to stay composed, but a few tears make it past my defenses.

"I miss you," I say. "I feel like I'm all by myself out here."

"Oh, baby, you're not alone. You've got family all around you."

"But they hate me, Mom. They don't want me here."

"I don't mean them, honey. I mean the ones who love you."

"Who loves me?" I take a seat on another bed close by. "I don't understand."

"He says you look just like her." She gets a familiar look in her eye, like she's trying to see through me. Apparently she can still have visions, even now. "They're coming..."

"Who's coming?" I wish I could take her hand. "Who's coming, Mom?"

"They're coming for you..." Fear contorts her features. "The man in chains. I didn't know what he was..."

"What man? Oh, God, Mom." It's like her final moments all over again. Incoherent scraps of thought and memory running together like watercolors.

"They took everything from us. But you're going to take it back. You have to be braver than I was. I couldn't help him then, but you can help him now."

"Who can I help?" I grip the stone lip beneath me to keep myself for reaching for her. "Mom, who's in chains?"

"Mariah," Keema says. She steps off the patio onto the garden path. "Is everything okay?"

When I turn to look back at my mother, her ghost is gone.

"No," I say, breathless.

"Are you feeling all right?" Keema asks, her face drawn with concern.

I wipe the tears from my cheeks. "I'm fine."

"You sure? I can get someone to cover if you need to take an hour off."

I shake my head. My mother's ghost is here. If I stay, there's a chance I'll see her again.

"I'm sure," I tell Keema. "I just thought I saw someone."

11

WILLIAM

"You were right, Will," Mariah says to me. "My mom is here. I saw her in the garden at work this morning."

"Did she recognize you?" I cross my feet on the dining table. Sadly, I missed their little mother-daughter reunion, thanks to Chastity choosing this fine morning to tap my arms like backyard maples.

"I wasn't sure at first, but yes, she did." She smiles to herself. "I wanted to hug her so badly. She looked so healthy."

Mariah picks a grape from the bunch on the cheese board in front of her. We're seated across from each other, at either end of the dining table, with an array of appetizers and half-eaten dishes spread out between us. Leftovers of a meal that was never actually served but exists to give the illusion of an ongoing gathering. The food is technically edible, if not at all nourishing.

Chastity passes through the dining room on her way to the kitchen. Mariah drops her grape in surprise.

"She can't see you," I remind her. By now, Mariah's figured out that the twilight realm is a sort of alternate version of her world, rather than a place she's invented.

"I know," she says. "It's still unnerving."

She waits for Chastity to make her return pass with a glass of wine in one hand and the open bottle in the other.

"Will, do you watch me during the day?"

If I had a pulse, it would jump three stories.

"Only when you're doing something private or embarrassing." I say, half joking. In truth, I watch her all the time.

Hell, just a few hours ago, I stood by her bed and watched her pleasure herself. A better man might've walked away as soon as her clothes came off, but I'm not a man. Not anymore. And considering the decades of pain I've endured at her father's hand, I reserve the right to steal a few stray moments of pleasure where I can get them.

She eyes me shrewdly. "Is something wrong? You seem quiet."

"My apologies. I'll try to be more entertaining."

"That's not what I meant," she said. "I don't need you to entertain me. I'm only asking in case you want to talk about it."

"We are talking." I scrub my face and sigh. This little girl's too astute for her own good.

I've been walking a knife's edge since I learned Chastity was dosing her with extra blood in the mornings. Mariah's powers are developing faster than she can detect them. It's only a matter of time before the family takes notice, and once they do, it'll be too late. She won't be trusted to move about the house unobserved.

However, more concerning than Mariah's budding abilities is my own hesitation. Since I've begun drawing her closer, I've been haunted by the specters of some highly inconvenient emotions.

At first, they took the form of admiration. I'd be in the middle of teasing her, like a cat with a mouse, and realize I was genuinely smiling. A smile brought on by something she'd said, or the way she threw her arms up while we danced.

During the day, when I'd normally park myself in the field, I would instead seek out her physical presence. If Chastity snapped at her, I'd allow myself the imagined satisfaction of biting out the other woman's tongue. If I noticed Edward eyeing her a second too long, I'd position myself in front of her—not that either of them could see me. I just couldn't abide the thought of him looking at her.

This desire to shelter Mariah from those who would harm her is bothersome at least and counterproductive at worst.

But what came next, I can't even account for.

Guilt. Like a cord tied around my ribcage, jerking me back when I should be inching closer.

I've killed innocents. It's all but guaranteed that I'll kill many more, especially if I remain at the vineyard. Mariah is just a human, alluring as she may be. Once she's freed me, I know the bloodlust will run its course, but this guilt I feel for deceiving her is a weakness I can't afford.

Mariah rises to stand at the window. I trace her shapely silhouette with my gaze before getting up to join her.

"I am sorry," I say. "It's been a long day."

"Whenever I find myself back here, it feels like I'm returning to the same long day." She looks at me. "I just want to help you."

"What if I told you there was a way you could help me?"

I stroke her chin.

"I'd say, tell me what it is, and I'll do it."

I could tell her to go to her father's study and steal the keys right now. I could say there's a poor, defenseless creature in the basement that needs to be rescued. It would all be done in a matter of minutes. The theft, my release, and her inevitable death.

But once again, that bastard guilt yanks at the cord around my chest like a rider pulling on reins.

She tilts her face upward. She wants me to kiss her, and I'm running out of excuses not to give her what she wants. What we both want...if I'm being honest.

Memories of another man stealing kisses from a young girl in the shadows of this estate flash in my mind like strobe lights. I take a step back from Mariah and rub my eyes, wiping the images away like rain from a windshield.

"What is your deal, Will?" Mariah asks, exasperated. "Do you want me or not? Because you're giving me some seriously mixed messages." She touches my arm. "Is it my age? My birthday's only two weeks away—"

My laughter slices between us like a knife cutting through cake. "You think a few days would make a difference in the face of half a millennium?"

She clasps her hands in front of her. "I guess not."

To hell with guilt, I tell myself. I'm tired of resisting temptation that insists on staring me in the face. I move in close, backing her up against the window.

"Mariah, if I wanted you on your back with your legs spread before me, your age would be the last thing standing in my way. If I wanted to sit on your bed and watch you play your pussy like a fiddle in the dark, completely oblivious to my presence, I could do that, too."

Her chest rises and falls, rises and falls. "But you haven't."

"Haven't I? How would you know?"

She swallows, and the contraction of her throat muscles is enough to make my gums tingle.

"Are you making fun of me?" she asks.

"I'm toying with you," I say. "There's a difference."

"It doesn't feel different." Her face glows with embarrassment. She thinks I'm going to all this trouble to prove that I don't want her. Because if I did, I'd have had her already, and the fact that I haven't is proof of my indifference.

If she knew how badly I wanted her, she'd be petrified. Like a puppy dashing after a tiger, she'd catch me and immediately regret giving chase.

"If you don't want me, you can just say so," she says. "You don't have to be an asshole about it."

I cradle the back of her neck and press my lips to hers.

Mariah tenses up, startled, then launches herself fully into the kiss. Her palms glide up my chest. I rest my hand on her waist and draw her close to feel her heat. As my tongue breaches her lips, she lets out a whimper that has my astral body humming like a plucked cello string.

I pull back to give her a chance to breathe.

"I didn't know ghosts could kiss like that," she whispers, her fingers closing around my shirt like she's afraid I'm going to slip away.

"I told you, I'm not a ghost."

"What are you, then?"

The closest thing I can think of without telling her the truth is, "A demon."

"You're not a demon." She smiles. "You're my imaginary friend."

"Some demons pretend to be your friend just to get close to you."

I take her hand and guide her back toward the dining table.

"What if I'm simply lying to get closer to you?" I lift her onto the table, pushing plates and silverware aside. "What if my true intention is to pick you like a flower, rip out all your petals, and crush you beneath my heel?"

She gasps as I skim my fingers up her thighs, sliding her tee shirt higher.

"I think I might like to be crushed by you," she says.

Her arms go around my neck as I kiss her again. Standing between her legs, I let her feel my erection against her thigh. Fortunately, I can get hard and even jack off here in the twilight realm. In the early years, it wasn't a bad way to pass the time. But after a while, the futility of fucking myself became just another source of depression.

Watching Mariah in bed these past few nights brought those desires back with a vengeance. There was no tearing my eyes from her dancing fingers as they circled her sensitive clit. I couldn't help imagining how it would feel to slide inside her wetness. I haven't been able to think about much else since.

"You've done this before?" I ask her.

She shakes her head. "But I really want to."

The fact that she's a virgin doesn't deter me. If anything, the thought of her dying before she's had a chance to be thoroughly ravished would be the real tragedy.

I lift her shirt up and off, baring her to my gaze. Her breasts are round and plump, her nipples tight and rosy. Beautiful, just like the rest of her. I kiss my way down from her jaw to her chest, careful not to linger too long at her neck. She moans as I lick her nipple, threading her fingers through my hair.

All of this is real, and yet, it isn't. Her pleasure is real. Her memory of my mouth on her breast and other places will be real, though her physical body remains untouched. Even so, she'll no doubt wake up with a desperate need to finger herself tomorrow.

I give her other nipple equal attention, as my hands curl around the band of her underwear. She lifts her bottom so I can pull them off, then whimpers as I kneel on the floor in front of her. She knows what's coming, even if she's only ever read about it, or whispered about the *other kind of kiss* with her friends at slumber parties.

The anticipation in her gaze makes my cock throb. If someone were to look at my physical body right now, they'd find me sporting a colossal hard on.

I kiss a line from her knee to her inner thigh. When my lips finally reach her pussy, she whimpers. I spread her wide so I can see all of her. My God, it has been far too long since I've come face-to-face with a woman's body, and hers is beyond luscious.

As I touch my tongue to her clit, I'm dismayed that my sense of taste is somewhat dulled in the twilight realm. Still, I can tell she's delicious. I don't want to waste a single drop of her honey.

I focus my attention on the tiny, stiffened bud that brings her so much pleasure. She moans, her heartbeat cantering along as I swirl my tongue against her. I try a few different approaches until I discern what she likes and then continue doing that until she's practically bucking.

As her breathing becomes erratic, I keep my pace consistent.

"Oh God, Will..." She tugs at my hair. "*Fuck...*"

I lick and suck her clit even as she shakes and twitches, until she goes still and silent, right before she moans.

As soon as she's finished riding out her orgasm, I stand and capture her open mouth. She tastes herself on me. Pulling her close, I grind my cock against her so there's no doubt in her mind how badly I want her. My hands map the landscape of her skin, just as her hands find and squeeze my ass.

"I want you," she whispers. "Please."

I feel almost lightheaded as I reach for the button on my pants. I haven't touched my own cock in years. Pulling it out, it becomes a hard, demanding thing between us that commands Mariah's attention. She wraps her fingers around the shaft. I groan.

"Your eyes are glowing," she says. I close them.

"Does it frighten you?"

"No," she says.

I kiss her hard. Thrusting into her fist, I feel like I could come from this slight contact alone. It's not the same as if she were touching my physical body, but it's a thousand times better than my own fist. Yes, I could indeed come just like this—

But I'm dying to get inside her.

As I grasp my cock to angle it toward her pussy, an image of Edward flashes across my vision.

I squeeze my eyes shut. Is he close to my body? I don't sense him nearby.

Another flash. This time it's Edward and Isabella as they were twenty years ago. I see Edward finding Isabella in the stables, backing her up against the stall. Edward whispering something into her ear. The two of them fucking on the hay-strewn floor...

I hold my head with both hands.

"Stop it," I growl.

"Why?" Mariah asks, letting go of my cock. "What's wrong?"

Another flash. Edward driving Mariah up to the house. Edward taking her hand. Mariah smiling at her father. Him watching her at dinner, at work, every chance he gets.

Watching and waiting for a sign that she can give him what he desires.

Money. Power. A future free of limitations.

"I can't..." I retreat from her until my back slams against the wall.

Mariah hops off the table and rushes to take my hands. As we touch, I see another flash: Edward caressing Mariah's face. Edward spreading her legs. Edward kissing her, touching her, in all the ways I've kissed and touched her.

There's no difference between what Edward has done, what he intends to do, and my own plans for his daughter. In this moment, we are the same person, working toward the same end.

Our freedom in exchange for hers.

"Will," she says. I evade her grasp faster than I mean to. She gasps. "How did you move so fast?"

She stares at me, incredulous, as I leave her—

I return to my physical body, gasping and coughing, a heap of bones barely holding together on the concrete floor.

My chains feel heavier than they did this morning. The braces around my neck and limbs burn.

"Sorry to intrude on your little date," Katherine says, "but I thought you should know that Mariah's boss told Edward about yesterday's episode in the garden."

I turn my head in the direction of Katherine's voice. My night vision isn't as good as it should be, so I can only discern her faint outline through the bars.

"You put those visions in my head," I croak.

"I showed you what you already know," she says. "The conclusions you've drawn are your own."

"If you weren't already dead, I'd fucking kill you."

"You were never going to go through with it, William. You know why you can't." She whirls around and exits through the exterior door.

Alone in the darkness, I open my mouth to roar, but all that comes out of my dry, cracked throat is another hacking cough.

12

MARIAH

I slide to my knees in front of the place where Will disappeared, my sweat gone cold and clammy from fear. He told me once that I look like incense burning when I leave him, and that's how he looked to me. I didn't think ghosts had anywhere to disappear to. Maybe there's a deeper level to this plane I don't know about. One that I can't reach.

I refuse to believe Will's a demon. My mom thought she met a demon once. He tried talking to her from inside her head, and it scared her so much she was afraid to be alone in a room for weeks.

Will doesn't scare me. He's more like my guardian angel, watching over me. I hope he's okay, wherever he's gone. As far as I know, there isn't anything that can permanently harm a spirit. Still, before he vanished, he looked like he was in a lot of pain.

I keep an eye out for Will on the property the next day, hoping I might spot him in the bleed-through. In my dreams, I search the house and the grounds and come up empty. I try to get down to the basement, but the door is locked, and I can't find a key.

A week passes, and I still can't find him.

It's like he's disappeared without a trace, not that Will has ever left much of a mark on the landscape. But on the map of my memory, he's a bright, shining beacon guiding me through the darkness.

Now his light is missing, and I don't know which way is north.

Where did you go, Will? Why won't you come back to me?

Edward stops me on my way out the door one morning to invite me to join the family for breakfast. It's Saturday, one of our busier days at the winery, and I'm finally running on time for a change, but he insists.

"I already told Keema I'd be keeping you this morning," he says. "I promise, you're going to want to see this."

I've been successfully avoiding Chastity and her mystery cocktails for a few days now. Whatever she has for me this morning, I'm not sure I can stomach it.

Swallowing a sigh, I say, "Okay, just for a minute," and follow Edward into the dining room where Chastity and Christopher are already seated.

"Look what I caught in the hall," Edward says.

Chastity bares her teeth. "How good of you to join us, Miss Greyson."

"Morning," I say.

Christopher fills his mouth with soggy-looking Grape-Nuts and says nothing. He's once again taken to glaring at me when he thinks Edward won't notice.

I take a seat, upturn my coffee mug, and reach for the pot of coffee at the center of the table. Chastity plops a glass of something deep purple in front of me.

"It's a blood-orange blueberry smoothie," she says.

"Thanks," I tell her. "But I'll just have coffee."

She squints. "But you need your vitamin C."

I grab an orange from the bowl of fruit on the table.

"I'll take this to work with me." I attempt to scoot my chair back. Edward rests his hand on my shoulder to stop me.

"Just a second." He sets a stack of dusty, old-looking photo albums on the table. I gasp.

"Are these my family's albums?" I ask.

"They are," he says. "Chastity had the maid look for them."

I meet Chastity's look of annoyance with a grateful smile. "Thank you so much."

"You're very welcome, Miss Greyson," she says. "They really were such a bother to locate. The poor maid with her asthma, coughing and sputtering all over the attic like a dying car engine." I wouldn't put it past her to have intentionally sought out an asthmatic maid for the job.

I make room for the albums in front of me and begin paging through, in order, from top to bottom. The earliest photos seem to date back to the twenties.

"Seen any familiar faces around the estate?" Edward asks. "Chastity's convinced the house is haunted. At least, that's her reasoning for why she's always knocking over her wineglasses."

He winks at Chastity, who purses her lips. I scan the faces for Will, and end up recognizing a few others, like the couple I saw outside the conservatory the first night I stayed here.

I figure there's no point in covering up my abilities anymore, since Edward is already convinced of their existence.

"I've seen them." I point out the couple from the first night, plus a few more from the party.

"Astonishing." Edward grins. "I knew you had the Greyson gift."

"Yes, how exciting," Chastity says. "Our very own psychic medium. Maybe you can read my palm sometime."

"I could try." Palm lines have their own objective meanings, but my mom was especially good at interpreting them. She'd sometimes get visions in the middle of a palm or tarot reading, though she refused to charge money for reconnecting people with dead loved ones. It felt exploitative.

In the next album, I find a photo taken in the dining room of a group of teenagers. At the center, in front of a large cake, stands a younger version of the woman I saw on the stairs. She's wearing a halter-style dress held up by a wide dark ribbon. Her hair is tied in twin braids. I tease the photo out of its sleeve and turn it over. Written on the back in perfect penmanship are the words, *Katherine Elenore Greyson, age 19, Happy Birthday*.

"She looks a lot like you," Edward says from over my shoulder.

"She's my grandmother. This photo was taken just three years before she died."

One of my grandpa's biggest regrets was leaving the estate without insisting on taking a few photo albums. According to him, Edward had demanded they leave the property immediately, giving Grandpa and my mom barely enough time to pack two small suitcases and be gone. When my grandpa called a few days later to inquire about the albums, Edward reminded him that he'd sold the estate with all of its contents, including photographs.

In a way, Edward showing me these albums now feels like he's trying to make amends for holding my family's history hostage. Unfortunately for my mom and grandpa, it's too little too late.

The first photo inside the last album is my mother's high school portrait. I trace the outline of her smiling face with my fingertip.

"She's so pretty," I say.

"Isabella was very beautiful," says Edward.

I don't even have to look at Chastity to know she's scowling, and I can't rightly blame her. What the hell is Edward thinking, saying something like that in front of his wife? I turn the page and find a bunch of photos taken at a Halloween party. My mother is dressed as Dorothy from *The Wizard of Oz*, complete with ruby-red heels and a fluffy toy dog in a basket.

"I remember that party," Edward says. "Isabella spent days decorating the stables. She invited all her girlfriends to the guesthouse for a sleepover."

"What guesthouse?" I wasn't aware there was one on the property.

"It's on the east side of the vineyard," Edward says, "tucked back into the trees. Chastity uses it as an office now, but your mother and grandfather lived there for a short while, after we bought the estate."

I wonder why Will never bothered to take me there all those nights we spent searching for my mother.

Edward turns the page for me and smiles at another photo of my mother in her Dorothy costume. "She looked especially lovely that night—"

"Oops!" Chastity's hand shoots out, knocking over the smoothie, and splattering purple liquid all over the photo album.

"So sorry about that," she says, clutching her necklace in a way that makes it crystal clear she's not sorry at all.

My heart cracks into pieces like a glass that's been dropped on the floor. I move like a thing possessed, rising from my seat and reaching across to slap Chastity across the face.

She yelps. We stare at one another for a handful of heartbeats, her in disbelief, and me in my fury.

"How dare you," I say. "These are the only photos I have of my mother when she was my age."

"Edward," Chastity says, "did you see what she just did to me?"

"What'd you expect, my dear?" he says, his voice as calm as a lake. "If you pull a cat's tail, don't be surprised when you get scratched."

"If a cat scratched me, I'd put it down."

Christopher's gaze jumps between his father and me, like he's waiting for something to happen. I suddenly feel like a mouse trapped in a maze, being watched by scientists in lab coats.

I attempt to sop up as much of the smoothie as possible using my napkin, as well as any others I can reach. Unfortunately, unlike newer albums with plastic barriers, these photos are only held in by paper slots at the corners.

I fetch a wad of paper towels from the kitchen, then begin laying down pieces between the dampened pages, praying at least a few of the photos will be salvageable. I re-stack the albums and clutch them to my chest.

"I don't know what kind of fucked-up games you're playing with each other," I say. "But keep me and my family out of them."

13

MARIAH

K eema offers to let me store the photo albums in her office during my shift. Part of me wants to say fuck it and hop on the next flight home, where the house I grew up in is waiting for me. But if my mom's ghost is here, along with both my grandparents, is that house really my home, or is this where I'm supposed to be?

The thought of calling anywhere the Radcliffs live *home* curdles my stomach.

And what about Will? I can't just leave without saying goodbye or finding out if he's okay.

I keep my head down and focus on work, trying not to think about where Will might be. If I close my eyes, I can still feel his hands on my body. His mouth performing pleasure spells between my thighs.

It seemed so real, his hunger for me. I felt it in the way he kissed me, in the way his hands roamed across my skin, mapping unchartered territory. He may not have touched my body, but he sure as hell left his mark on my psyche.

Falling for a ghost has to be one of the most painful things you can do to yourself. It can only end in heartbreak. But after everything I've been through this year—all the pain and loss—I feel like maybe fate owes me a small bite of happiness. I'm not asking for much. Just a chance to forget about the real world for a few hours, with a man who looks at me like I'm best thing that's happened to him in centuries.

Halfway through my shift, our most seasoned sommelier, Burt, asks me to run to the basement for another bottle of Pinot. The tasting room has its own wine cellar, separate from the winery, where we keep the bottles specifically reserved for tours.

The light switch at the top of the staircase only illuminates the stairs below. You have to turn on the second switch at the bottom to see the shelves. As I grope the wall, I realize something's different. There's no light switch at the bottom, and the wall itself feels like it's made of stone instead of sheetrock.

I descend the last step and find the entire floor steeped in liquid. It oozes into the sides of my sandals, slick and warm.

Blood. At least an inch of it, deep red and glossy beneath the subtle glow of lantern light that shouldn't be here.

A long stone corridor stretches out before me. I've never seen this hallway before. It's like something you'd find in a dungeon or the basement of a building much older than this one.

I must be dreaming, I tell myself. But when did I fall asleep?

And if I am dreaming, where's Will?

Behind the door, something whispers, like the whoosh of an arrow over my shoulder.

A door appears at the end of the corridor, a heavy-duty metal thing with a serious-looking lock. I know instinctively that Will's behind it, and I want to go to him, but I'm scared.

Breathing deeply, I force myself forward, one step a time, through the pool of blood that ripples as I move through it.

My pulse sprints. A low hum tickles my ears as I approach the door, growing louder and louder. Bees, I think at first, then no, not bees. *Voices.* Hundreds of voices, some urging me to keep going while others beg me to turn and run.

He's coming, they say. *He's coming... Find him... Save him...*

Run.

A bloody hand reaches out of the pool and grasps my ankle. I scream. Another hand rises up to grab me, and then another.

Half a dozen bloody arms reaching, grabbing, and dragging me to the floor.

My entire front body is soaked in blood. The taste of iron fills my mouth. I crawl toward the door on hands and knees, slipping. Splashing.

Blood in my eyes. In my nose.

The whispers become cries.

He's coming... Turn back... Go back...

A door slams.

I'm shrouded in darkness, breathing heavily on two feet.

My hands and clothes are dry, as is my mouth.

At the sound of footsteps on the stairs behind me, I turn.

Christopher flips the light switch—the one that wasn't there a few moments ago. I squint against the brightness, confused and grateful to be back in the tasting room's wine cellar.

"You look like you've seen a ghost," Christopher says, tucking his hands into his front pockets. "I figured you'd be used to that by now."

I shake my head, blinking away the mental cloudiness left over from...whatever the hell that was. Some kind of vision?

"I'm at work, Christopher. I don't have time to talk." I grab a bottle of Pinot from the shelf, then attempt to head upstairs. He refuses to budge from my path. "I have to get back."

"My father is determined to make you part of this family," he says. "Yet he holds you to a different standard than the rest of us. Tell me, how is that fair?"

"You'll have to ask Edward," I say, pretending to be more annoyed than nervous when he takes a step toward me. "Please move."

"Put down the bottle if you don't want to drop it."

I roll my eyes, even as my pulse flutters. "For fuck's sake, Christopher—"

"Put it down," he snaps.

My throat closes. I force my shoulders back, refusing to let on how fragile I feel. "Get out of my way, Christopher. I have work to do."

He grabs the wine bottle from me and lets it drop. Glass shatters.

Wine spreads out across the concrete and under my sandals. *Just like blood...*

I meet his cold gaze and my heart starts to riot in my chest. He takes another step. I move, and before I realize where I've brought myself, he's got me backed up against a set of shelves.

"Take off your apron," he says.

"No." He slams both hands on the shelves, penning me in. I flinch but stand my ground. "Get out of my face."

He grabs me by the shoulders. I push at his chest, but he's built like a fucking lumberjack. He turns me around, pressing his forearm to the back of my neck as he unties my apron himself. He tugs the back of my shirt up and over my head so I can't see. I brace my hands on the shelves and push with all my might, but he holds me firmly in place.

I don't understand how he can be this strong. It's like trying to fight a pick-up truck.

"My father might be too scared to punish you for slapping my mother, but I'm not."

"Your mother ruining those photos was punishment enough."

"I disagree." I hear the metallic clink of his belt, and my stomach clenches. He unhooks my bra with one hand —all those make-out session with private-school girls finally coming in handy, I'm sure.

"Christopher, please." I pray for Keema or one of the other tasting-room assistants to come downstairs. "Don't do this."

I recoil at the swish of his belt passing through the loops on his pants.

"You want to be a Radcliff?" he says. "Consider this your initiation."

His belt buckle hits my back like a stone. I cry out in pain.

"Shut the fuck up," he hisses.

Tears streak down my face as he hits me again.

My back is on fire. I lose count of how many times he beats me. My insides churn like an electrical storm, each blow a bolt of lightning streaking across my back. Even as the pain sears through me, part of me can't believe this is really happening. I ask myself, why didn't I fight harder? Why didn't I scream louder? What gives him the goddamn right to do this to me?

Shame and anger roil within me, like water boiling in a pot.

Bubbling and bursting until the lid can no longer stay on.

My screams are drowned out by the explosion of glass shattering around me. Wine bottles burst, spilling their ruddy contents to the floor.

Christopher staggers back. I can feel his shock, sense his panic. My consciousness swells until it's touching every corner of the room.

Then, as suddenly as it expanded, it retracts.

I push away from the shelves and take a deep, steadying breath. I'm still humming with psychic energy as I right my clothes, my back stinging from even the slight weight of my tee shirt.

Glancing around the room, I take in the destruction. Every single bottle that was on the shelf now lies shattered, the contents puddling into a mass of dark, red liquid on the floor.

Just like the blood in my vision.

What the hell is happening to me?

As I take a step toward Christopher, he jumps back, slipping and falling on his ass. He shouts as bits of glass floating in the wine embed themselves into the fat of his palms.

Everything seems to move in slow motion. Drops of blood falling from Christopher's hands, hitting the surface of the wine on the floor, rippling outward...

A wave of exhaustion crests, threatening to wash over me. The understanding that I don't have much time plants itself like a seed in my mind. I don't know where it comes from or what it means, but I know I don't want to be anywhere near Christopher when the wave hits.

I step over his legs on my way to the stairs. Right before I ascend, I glance over my shoulder to tell him, "Stay the fuck away from me."

Ditching my apron in Keema's office, I gather the photo albums and race out to the field where I first met Will. Soon enough, the wave of fatigue to comes crashing down on me, and I'm brought to my knees in the grass.

14

WILLIAM

I lie beside Mariah's sleeping body, waiting to feel the ping of her psychic presence somewhere on the estate. She clutches the albums to her chest like a child clinging to a stuffed animal. I can already see the deep-red bruising on her back through her white shirt.

It guts me that I can't draw her close and stroke her tear-tracked face. I saw what Christopher did to her. I was there. Howling and railing against it, my fists swiping straight through her half-brother's form.

It's one thing for them to hurt me. I expect and have even come to accept it as part of my lot. But to watch them leave marks on Mariah, to hear her agonizing cries and be unable to do a damn thing to stop them... I've never felt more impotent as a man or as a monster.

But what she did with those wine bottles was nothing short of astounding.

I've heard stories about human psychics who were strong enough to channel their anger with that much intensity, but never witnessed it myself. From the look of surprise on her face, it appears the destruction was entirely accidental.

Imagine what she could accomplish with a few years of conscious practice under her belt.

"You are more powerful than you know," I whisper, though she cannot hear me.

I feel her manifest on the road to the winery and rush over to meet her. When she catches sight of me a few yards ahead of her, she stops and stares.

I walk toward her, and she starts running. She jumps, throwing her arms and legs around me, and I catch her, cradling her bottom in my palms. I kiss her long and hard, like a dying man who's just found water in the desert. Her legs tighten around my hips as she meets my enthusiasm head on.

"Where've you been?" she asks, breathless.

"Closer than you think."

"But I couldn't find you."

I smooth her hair away from her face.

"I just needed some time, and a little space to think." Time to face my own delusions and mourn the loss of hope. Space to embrace the inevitable: that I will never escape the prison her father has trapped me in.

"Space?" Her body tenses. "In the movies, when guys say they need space, they mean they want to date other girls."

I curse myself for staying away for as long as I did. Time flows differently on this side of the coin. Three days in the physical world can pass like an hour in the twilight realm. I kiss her cheeks.

"There are no other girls, Mariah. I'm sorry I disappeared on you. It won't happen again." It's a promise I feel comfortable making, because unless Edward kills me, I literally cannot break it.

She releases her hold on my hips, sliding both feet to the ground. "What happened to you? Where'd you go?"

I press my forehead to hers, trying to recall the memory of her taste on my tongue, without also summoning the awful visions that haunted me.

"I remembered something that upset me very much," I tell her.

"What did you remember?"

I shake my head. "It doesn't matter."

I kiss her again. Normally, she wouldn't let me get away with dodging her questions, but she's enjoying the kiss too much to make me stop.

Her hand brushes my cock. I inhale sharply and force myself to back off. It's a gargantuan effort that I didn't know I was capable of.

"Easy, tiger," I say. "I saw what happened to you in the wine cellar. Are you all right? Do you want to talk about it?"

She frowns like I've just dumped water all over her campfire.

"Do I look like I want to talk about it?"

Her eyes glimmer with unshed tears. I pull her close as they start to fall.

"I tried to push him off me," she whispers. "He was so strong."

"So were you," I say. "What you did to those wine bottles was incredible."

"I don't know how I did it." She takes a shuddering breath. "All that glass, the wasted wine. I didn't mean to make a mess."

"Don't give it a second thought." I meet her gaze. "You were defending yourself."

She nods. "What's happening to me, Will?"

"I don't know." But I do know someone who could help guide her through it.

I kiss her again and then take her by the hand. "Come on, I want you to meet someone."

"Who?" she asks. "Where are we going?"

"Somewhere I should've brought you a long time ago."

I've been avoiding taking Mariah to the guesthouse where Katherine and John spend most of their time, helping Isabel come to terms with her death. It's also the place where Chastity stores large quantities of my blood, before she and Edward slip it into the wine after the workers clock out.

Unlike human blood, vampire blood doesn't separate, and it stays fresh a great deal longer if kept cold. Chastity keeps the guesthouse locked down like Fort Knox. But here in the twilight realm, Katherine could, in theory, open one of the refrigerator doors and show Mariah the stores of my blood.

Mariah remains convinced that I'm a ghost. Once she learns the truth about what I am and what Edward intends to do to her, there's a good chance she'll run screaming. Best case scenario, Mariah runs as far away from this place as she can, tonight. Before it's too late.

I've accepted the inevitability of her loss, as I've accepted the fact that I cannot consciously sacrifice her to free myself. Driving her away is the only option, because even if I do nothing, I will end up killing her regardless.

Edward was supposed to feed me yesterday. He never showed. I am weak and famished, which means by the time he drags Mariah down to the cellar, I will have no control over my impulses.

There is still time to save her, but I have to act fast.

I guide her down the winding dirt drive that leads through a patch of woods on the edge of the estate. It's dark within the trees, and she squeezes my hand as we move deeper into the forest. I kiss her knuckles. As we round the bend, we come upon the guesthouse, its windows glowing with lamplight. Having been built in the late fifties, the architecture is modern compared to that of the main house.

The front door opens at our approach, and Isabella steps out. Mariah gasps. They run toward each other, pulling one another into a tight embrace.

"I've missed you so much," Isabella says, remarkably composed for a spirit who croaked barely a month ago.

John and Katherine step out of the house. Mariah beams at the sight of her grandfather and rushes to hug him. He swings her around like a child, then sets her down to get a good look at her.

He introduces her to her grandmother, who smiles shyly. I don't think I've ever seen Katherine so nervous. It's unnerving, like seeing a dog walk on its hind legs. She reaches out to touch Mariah's face. Mariah smiles warmly as grandmother and granddaughter embrace.

I wait patiently on the small patch of lawn, letting this belated reunion play out as it's meant to. Mariah is the happiest I've ever seen her, and I know I deserve all the pain Edward can pitch at me and then some for denying her this happiness these past few weeks.

John ushers the women into the house. Katherine pauses in the doorway.

"Come inside, William," Katherine says.

I expect to feel out of place among the family, but watching Mariah interact so easily with the people she loves fills me with a warmth I haven't felt since I was a very young vampire among my brothers.

Isabella is cooking something on the stove that I can't smell. I'm willing to bet she can't smell it either, but old habits die harder than the body.

The interior of the guesthouse is decorated in a distinctly sixties fashion. However, I can see through the twilight's veneer to the physical, modern décor underneath, including the refrigerators that house my blood.

"Grandpa and I are going on a short walk," Mariah says, squeezing my hand. "He wants to show me some night-blooming moonflower not far from here." She kisses my cheek and whispers, "Thank you for bringing me here."

I nod, fearing it's all too little too late.

John and Mariah head outside, leaving me to contend with Katherine and Isabella on my own.

Katherine takes a seat in one of the armchairs, while Isabella fusses over whatever she's pretending to make on the stove. Seeing the two of them together is a head trip. Having died so young, Katherine looks like she could be her daughter's daughter.

"I know why you've brought her here," Katherine says. "And I'm afraid we can't help you."

"She has to leave tonight," I say.

"She won't," Isabella says. "Your bringing her here has ensured that. She knows her family is here now. This is her home."

"They're going to kill her."

Katherine smirks. "Meaning, you're going to kill her for them."

I clench my jaw, biting back a groan. "Isn't there something you can do?"

"Mariah is on a path she must walk all the way down," Isabella says. "As are you."

Katherine glances at her daughter. "Indeed."

"But you could show her the blood stores," I tell Katherine. "Help me prove to her that I'm not a ghost. Show her what Edward plans to do with her—"

"It won't matter, William," Katherine says. "You know what I've seen. She will find out what you are soon enough. If you try to tell her now, she won't believe you."

"Mariah must die," Isabella says. "It can't be avoided."

"With all due respect," I say, "how is Isabella even capable of having this conversation?"

"My baby's always been a fast learner." Katherine smiles proudly. They share a tender look between them that makes me want to smash their heads together.

"Glad to see you're all on-board with the prospect of Mariah's impending death," I say.

"An amusing accusation, coming from you," says Katherine. "I would've thought you'd be the happiest of all of us to have her trapped here with you forever."

"Not if it means killing her." And losing the ability to touch her, I think, but decide not to say aloud.

"What happened to doing whatever it takes to get your revenge?" Katherine asks.

I sigh heavily, running a hand down my scruff. "I would rather Mariah escape this place and live a full, happy life, far from here, than to have her stuck on the estate, surrounded by her father's family."

Isabella offers me a bowl of something I can neither eat nor touch. I wave my hand through the dish.

"If you think my daughter will love you any less once she learns what you are and what you've been through, then you don't regard her as highly as you claim to." She stares at me for a long moment, no doubt flipping through visions of my future like pages in a picture book.

I clear my throat. "Can we please focus on the present?"

"You doubt your love for her, Will," she says. "You shouldn't. Love is the most powerful force there is. It makes us stronger, not weaker."

"A few weeks ago, he would've argued that vengeance was the stronger motivator," Katherine says.

Isabella cocks her head. "Now he's not so sure."

"I didn't think William was capable of loving anyone but himself."

"He is capable of loving her," Isabella says. "But his is not a sweet love, or a kind love. His love will drag her to her knees and slice through her like a knife, before it rips her heart out."

They regard me with contempt, despising me for a crime I haven't yet committed—a crime I seem to be the only one interested in trying to prevent.

Isabella shudders. "Please step outside, Will. I can't bear to look at you right now."

"Please." I implore both of them. "I'm begging you—"

"Go," Katherine says.

I march out of the house, exasperated and dismayed. This is precisely why I've always avoided the company of witches. Haughty wenches talk over and around you like they have all the answers, because they usually do. It's maddening. Though I'd bet the futility of being able to predict the future, while lacking the ability to change it, would drive anyone mad eventually.

I wait on the steps for Mariah and her grandfather to return. When I catch sight of them coming up the drive, I stand. She thanks John for showing her the flowers, hugs him, then waits for him to go inside before wrapping her arms around me. I kiss her like it's the last time I'll get the chance to—because it very well might be.

"I can't believe they're all here," she says. I press my lips to her forehead. There's tension in her muscles, and I know the question she wants to ask before she's even said it. "Will, why did you wait so long to bring me here?"

"I was worried your family would warn you away from me."

"Why would they do that?"

"Because I'm not a ghost," I tell her. "I'm a vampire. Edward's got me locked in a cage, and he and Chastity have been stealing my blood to add to their wines. I wanted to trick you into freeing me so I could drink your blood and escape."

Mariah stares at me like I've just sprouted a second head.

"Is that supposed to be a joke?" she asks. "Because it's a bad one."

I cradle her face in my hands. It's too late to save us both, but I can take one last shot at saving her. If there was ever a time for Katherine's vision to be wrong, I pray it's now.

"Mariah, I need you to listen to me. My blood is in the wine. It's what triggered your powers, and now Edward wants to turn you into a vampire so he can steal your blood like he's stolen mine. He thinks you're clairvoyant, like your mother, and he wants that power for himself."

"Will..." She shakes her head. "You're confused."

"I'm not confused. I'm trying to save your life." This is too much for her right now, but she needs to hear it, and I have to say it because Isabella's right.

I do love Mariah, more than anything.

I don't know when it happened exactly. Sometime between our first dance and our first kiss. She got under my skin, and from there, my love for her grew like vines around the trellis of my ribs.

There's no point in trying to fight or deny it. I love her, and I'm willing to risk sounding like a madman to save her.

"You have to get as far away from here as possible," I tell her.

"Will, my family's here. *You're* here. I'm not leaving either of you."

"You have to." I grasp her shoulders. "Edward is coming for you—"

"Even if that one part of this insane story is true, I can take care of myself. You saw what I did to the wine, to Christopher."

"It won't matter. If you stay here, you will die. He will force me to kill you."

She takes a step back. "Will, you're scaring me."

"You should be scared." I don't want to do this, but I have no choice. She needs to see the truth with her own eyes.

Focusing on my gums, I will my fangs to extend.

Mariah's eyes widen. She gasps.

"This isn't funny, Will. Stop it."

"Do I look like I'm joking?" I move forward, faster than her eyes can detect, until I'm looming over her. "This is what will happen if you don't leave tonight. Only, next time, you won't wake up."

I hate myself for what I'm about to do to her but biting her now won't kill her or even leave scars. Not physical ones, at least. I won't blame her one bit if she never wants to see me again after this—

Pain shoots up my arms, sharp and debilitating. At first, I think it's Katherine trying to stop me from biting Mariah. Then I realize the pain's stemming from my physical body.

I've been so distracted that I didn't even notice Edward's approach.

Mariah calls my name and it sounds like she's standing at the other end of a long tunnel.

I come back to myself, chained to the stone wall, two very thick needles shoved into my veins, and the rim of a metal cup jammed into my mouth.

"As I suspected," Edward says, continuing a conversation I'm only now becoming a part of. "Milking venom from a vampire really isn't all that different from milking it out of a snake."

I bite down on the metal cup, puncturing it. Edward rips the cup away.

"That's enough," he says. "I only needed a few drops, anyway." He pours my saliva into a small glass tube, then caps it. "So sorry for the delay in feeding. I won't have a fresh one for you for a few days."

I can smell the bags of donor blood he's brought with him. They're slightly past their prime, but even so, I salivate. I know exactly who he intends to drag in here in a few days, just in time for her eighteenth birthday.

"She won't turn," I croak. He shoots me one of his signature how-the-hell-did-you-guess looks. "I'll drain her dry before I let you have her."

"You think I'm just going to throw her in here with you and wait for nature to take its course?" Edward chuckles. "Turning is a science, William, much like winemaking. I wouldn't toss a bunch of random grapes in a barrel and call it Merlot, and I'm not stupid enough to let you anywhere near my investment."

He switches out a full jar of my blood for an empty one. I'm surprised I have enough in me to fill one jar, let alone multiples.

Maybe he's finally decided to bleed me to death.

My gaze falls to the vial of my saliva on the table. If Edward can get my venom into Mariah's system before he kills her, he could facilitate her turning without involving me at all.

It would be a far cleaner, and more efficient way to accomplish his goal.

And Edward is nothing if not efficient.

I close my eyes in defeat.

"All these years, I've wondered how long it would take for a vampire to starve to death," he says. "Perhaps, one of these days, if my investment pays off, you and I will get to find out."

15

MARIAH

My grandmother places a plastic thimble at the center of the kitchen table.

"See if you can call it to you," she says.

I focus my attention on the thimble. It trembles and tips over. I'm so startled by the movement that I lose my concentration. It rolls to the edge of the table and falls to the floor.

"That was good," she says. My grandmother is very impressed by my ability to manipulate objects with my mind, both here in the spirit realm and in the real world.

"Try again," my mom says. I sigh.

"I don't understand how I managed to blow up an entire cellar full of wine, but I can't even make a thimble roll my way." Edward blamed the broken bottles and lost product on a small earthquake and shoddy construction.

I'm not sure if he knows what really happened, or who he was trying to cover for. He hasn't said anything to me about it, though I haven't exactly made myself available to the Radcliffs since the incident with the photo albums.

"Trauma and necessity are powerful triggers," my grandmother says. "But smaller tasks require specific intent. Keep practicing."

She places the thimble back on the table. I take a deep breath and try again.

Things haven't been the same between Will and I since he bared his fangs to me. Instead of immediately running to meet him in the vines as soon as I arrive in the spirit realm, I head to the guesthouse to say hello to my family. After visiting with them for a while, my mom walks me out to the fields.

Will keeps his hands to himself for the most part or holds mine chastely as we walk about the vineyard. He looks at me like he knows something terrible is going to happen, and I hate it.

I want us to go back to the way we were, when I thought I was falling in love. I do love him. That hasn't changed. But the fear he instilled in me that night lingers in my body like muscle memory.

Maybe he really is a demon, and I just didn't want to believe it.

"How come I still can't see the future?" I ask my mom. We are on our way to the edge of the field where Will usually waits for me, but he isn't there. It's the middle of the day, so he's probably not expecting me. I don't often take naps in the afternoon, but today's birthday, and I wanted to spend it with my real family.

"Maybe you will someday," she says. "For whatever reason, right now, your powers are manifesting differently. Honestly, sweetheart, it'll be a blessing if you don't inherit the sight. It breaks your heart far more often than it helps you."

"Will thinks Edward is planning something terrible for me."

"Edward is always cooking up some grand plan," she says.

I stop walking. "Mom, is Will a ghost?"

She gazes pensively out at the vines.

"Mom, for once, just be straight with me, please."

She takes my hand in hers. "Will told you what he is."

"So, he really is a demon? Or a vampire? Is there even a difference?"

"I don't know." I figure that's all I'm going to get out of her, but then she says, "You have to be brave, sweetheart. Use your gifts. Don't let Will's doubt convince you it's hopeless. He doesn't remember how to hope. You have to remind him."

The wind plays with our hair.

"You know what's coming," I say. "Tell me."

"Will already told you." She pets my cheek with sadness in her eyes. "Happy birthday, baby. I'll see you soon—"

Knocking. Loud and swift.

I open my eyes to the dimly lit room. The horizon out my open window is peachy pink. It's a perfectly crisp October evening. At first, I'm not sure whether I'm asleep or awake. Then the knocking resumes. I roll out of bed and rub the sleep from my eyes, then open the door and wish I could close it again.

"I hope you know the only reason I let you nap all afternoon is because it's your birthday," Chastity says, her expression pinched. After the incident with the smoothie, she and I have successfully been avoiding each other, until now. "Dinner's going to be served in the conservatory. It's your special night, so dress accordingly."

I thank her curtly and shut the door, wishing I could crawl back into bed. I hate that I have to share this place with my father's family. If I could sleep forever and live out the rest of my life in the spirit realm, I'd do it in a heartbeat.

I shower quickly and slip into Edward's birthday gift to me, a red, beaded-lace dress. He surprised me with it this morning after breakfast, with a card that read, *A special occasion deserves a special dress. Happy Birthday.*

As I enter the conservatory, I'm met by the warmth of hundreds of twinkling lights strung around the room. Even some of the plants have been wrapped in string lights. I'm surprised to see Lilliana seated at the table, back from school on a weeknight. She eyes my dress with tepid interest.

"Happy birthday, Mariah," Edward says, as he enters the conservatory. He takes my hand and spins me so he can see the full effect of the dress he bought. "I knew red was your color. You look absolutely stunning."

"Thanks," I say. He pulls out my chair for me, and I sit down. The skin on the back of my neck prickles. I stroke my nape. Something doesn't feel right, or maybe it's me that doesn't feel right. Either way, I wish Will were here right now.

A moment later, we're joined by Christopher and Chastity. Edward pulls the cork from an unlabeled bottle of wine and pours me a glass. I watch the deep red liquid swish around the bowl, and my throat tightens.

"The birthday girl gets a special vintage," Edward says.

I smile tightly, remembering what Will said about there being blood in the wine.

Edward stands at the head of the table and raises his glass. I brace myself for what I'm sure will be another uncomfortable toast.

"I can't tell you how much joy it brings me to have my whole family here tonight," Edward says. "This place wouldn't be the same without all of your efforts."

I keep my smile pasted on as Edward rambles on about legacy and things we leave behind. Glancing around the table, I catch three sets of eyes staring back at me. I feel like a clue under a microscope, like the key to something bigger than me.

"Mariah," Edward says, "getting to know you has been a privilege. I'm sorry you had to come under such tragic circumstances, but I hope the beauty and splendor of this place has helped ease the pain of your loss. You're eighteen now and your old house is now in your name. While I'm certain Baltimore is ripe with fond memories for you, I think Isabella would want you to stay. Personally, I hope to have you with us for a very long time," he says. I shiver. "Cheers."

We lift our glasses. As soon as the wine touches my tongue, I taste it.

Copper. Iron. Blood.

Will's blood.

I drop my glass.

Chastity shrieks. "My tablecloth!"

Red sweeps across the white fabric like time-lapsed clouds rolling over a town. A bit of it even soaks into my dress. Edward's gaze follows the stain as it approaches him.

"I'm sorry," I say, my voice trembling. "It just slipped out of my hand."

"That's all right," Edward says. "I'll get you a fresh glass."

"Actually, I'll just have a soda."

"Of course." His smile is taut as he pushes back from the table.

Chastity stands. "I'll get it for her. I need to grab about five gallons of club soda while I'm at it."

Staff appears to help extricate the tablecloth. We begin eating. I sip my soda sparingly and eat my dinner quickly, hoping no one will notice the sweat beading on my upper lip.

Will was right about the wine, which means he's probably right about the rest of it. He's here somewhere, trapped.

A staff member clears my dinner plate and replaces it with a smaller one. Chastity sets a white cake down on the table. Candles are lit. There's a half-hearted attempt at a Happy Birthday sing-a-long. I blow out the candles, wishing to survive the night.

Edward hands me a knife. "Will you do the honors?"

"Sure." My hand shakes as I cut the first piece, and my heart stops as I lift the slice away from the rest of the cake, revealing a red-velvet center.

I taste blood in the cake. God knows how much blood I've consumed since I arrived at this place. I force myself to chew and swallow, feigning interest in Lilliana's classes and Christopher's upcoming lacrosse game.

After dessert, I'm brought to the library where I'm given presents to unwrap. A pale pink scarf from Lilliana. A Tori Amos CD I already own from Christopher. A set of scented candles and bubble bath from Chastity.

I thank them for the gifts and excuse myself to my room. As soon as I shut the door, I drag my suitcase from the closet and start piling my clothes inside.

Halfway through packing, I stop.

I can't just run away. If Will's caged somewhere on the property, I need to find him and free him. He said something about Edward forcing him to kill me. My head swims. I sit on the edge of the bed and concentrate on my breathing.

I can't seem to take a deep enough breath.

My limbs give out.

I'm on the floor.

My spirit manifests a few feet from my unconscious body. I gaze down at myself, confused. Did Edward drug me? I don't think I drank enough of the wine for whatever was in it to affect me. Maybe he put it in my food?

The doorknob clicks.

A voice hisses, "Is she passed out yet?"

Lilliana pokes her head into my room. "She's out."

Christopher slips in behind his sister and immediately shuts off the light. I watch, rooted in place, as he lifts my body into his arms without much effort.

"Did you see Dad on your way up?" Christopher asks.

"I just left him in his study," Lilliana says quietly. "Let's go."

They carry my body out of the room, shutting the door behind them. I follow.

Christopher almost hits my head against the wall twice on his way down the stairs. Lilliana hisses at him to be careful. Whatever they're doing, they clearly don't want Edward to know about it.

After passing through the foyer, they come to the door that leads to the cellar.

Lilliana pulls a heavy set of keys from her pocket and tries one. It doesn't work. She tries another. The door opens.

I trail them down the steps and stop short at the bottom of the staircase. Fear winds its way up my spine as I stare down the stone corridor from my vision at the winery.

Where the hell are these two taking me?

Lilliana hits a switch. Lanterns illuminate the way forward. They continue on, deeper and deeper into the darkness, finally coming to a stop in front of a familiar heavy-looking door. Lilliana begins testing out different keys.

"Mom said the big one opens the main door," Christopher says.

Of course Chastity would be in on it, I think. I bet she's the one who drugged me.

Heavy bolts clink and clang. Lilliana draws the metal door back, revealing a pitch-black interior. They carry me into the shadows. I move into the doorway just as Lilliana yanks it shut.

Fluorescent light fills every corner of the space, momentarily blinding me. Then, I see him.

At the center of a square cage, lies the naked body of an emaciated man. His skin is pale and stretched over his bones. His hair is messy and gray from dust. His face is wrinkled and blue.

I move closer, and it's not until I'm standing right up against the cage that I realize the withered figure I'm looking at is Will.

A hand grasps my wrist. I whirl around, and there he is. My Will. Looking vibrant and healthy.

He pulls me against him, and I immediately start sobbing.

"I'm sorry I didn't believe you," I say.

He shushes me softly. "It's all right. It's okay."

But it's not okay. None of this is okay.

Christopher lays me on the floor so he can stretch his arms. Lilliana pokes around a shelf containing what appears to be medical supplies.

"Is he still alive?" Christopher asks.

"Why don't you stick your hand in and find out." Lilliana sets the keychain down on a wide control panel sporting colorful buttons. I extricate myself from Will's embrace to go study the controls.

"What do they do?" I ask him.

"Regulate humidity and temperature, mostly," he says. "But they also control my chains."

I glance back at his body, noting the awful chains that run from the wall to the cuffs around his neck, wrists and ankles.

Lilliana opens a drawer and begins rummaging through its contents.

"What the hell are you looking for?" Christopher asks.

"Something sharp."

"You think he'll wake up if he smells her blood?"

"That's the idea," she says.

"I can already smell your blood," Will says to me. "It's taking all my remaining strength to continue projecting myself. I don't know how much longer I'll be able to stay here."

Lilliana opens another drawer and pulls out a scalpel.

"This'll work. Let's get her inside the cage." She pushes a button on the panel, and suddenly, Will's body is jerked back against the stone wall. He winces beside me. I squeeze his hand.

"Think he'll absorb her powers?" Christopher asks.

"Who cares," Lilliana says. "Dad's plan was always moronic. I mean, look at her. If she could predict the future, she wouldn't be here. So what if she can see her dead relatives? She doesn't have any useful powers."

My mother's words echo in my mind. *Use your gifts.* I let go of Will's hand and approach his body. The chains securing him didn't look particularly special, though the cuffs shine like they're coated with something.

"Why can't you rip off the cuffs?" I ask.

"They're coated with a silver alloy," he says. "Chronic exposure weakens me. The fact that I'm so malnourished doesn't help."

"How are they locked?"

"They're secured in place by silver-plated screws," he says. "You need a power drill to remove them."

A power drill, or a fuckton of psychic focus.

I study his arm, frowning at the dark marks on the inside of his elbow. This must be how they steal his blood. I crouch and examine the cuff mechanism.

"If I concentrate hard enough, I think I can remove the screws that hold the cuffs together," I tell him.

He shakes his head and turns me to face him. "No. You need to concentrate on getting the hell out of here. I'm going to wake you, and you're going to fight with everything you've got."

"Will, I can do this." I wince as Lilliana cuts into my wrist with the scalpel. Will's jaw clenches. He grasps my shoulders tightly, like he's fighting to stay on his feet. My blood must smell intoxicating to him.

"Drag her inside," Lilliana says.

Christopher balks. "I'm not going in there."

"He's chained to the wall. You'll be fine."

"If it's so safe, then you do it."

She rolls her eyes. "Fine."

Lilliana snatches up the keychain, then stops halfway to the cage, staring at Will's prone body. I use her hesitation to my advantage, turning my focus on the screw securing Will's left ankle cuff. It takes a couple of tries, but eventually, it starts to turn.

Will pulls on my arm. "Mariah, you have to wake up."

I shake him off.

"Not yet."

The screw is at least two inches in length, and badly tarnished. It twists and turns and twists some more, until it pops out onto the floor.

We stare at the fallen screw and wait for Lilliana and Christopher to notice, but they're too busy arguing over who's the bigger pussy.

"When'd you learn to do that?" Will asks.

"Just now." I focus on removing the screw from his right ankle, then his wrists. My head pounds as I struggle to work the final screw from his throat cuff.

Will wraps his arms around me from behind. I lean against him, throwing all of my focus into loosening the screw.

It falls to the floor.

"You're incredible," he says into my hair. "You know that?"

I smile. "Don't thank me just yet. We still have to get you out of this cage. Wait for one of them to drag me inside, then pounce."

"No. I'll rip you to pieces right alongside them. You have to get out first."

"If they don't open your cage then it was all for nothing." I kiss the inside of his palm. "I trust you, Will. Now I need you to trust yourself with me."

He kisses me, his hands grasping at my body like he's afraid to let go. But he needs to. Releasing the demon inside him is the only way he can free us both.

"Okay," he rasps. "But the second the bloodlust takes hold, I become a hunter. I won't be able to stop until my prey is dead."

"So, don't stop," I tell him. "Hunt them down."

Will's face hardens with renewed resolve. He searches my gaze for understanding and finds it. He's going to kill them all, and I'm going to let him do it.

There's a loud clang and the grinding of metal against metal. Lilliana has turned the key in the lock.

"The second you wake up," Will says, "crawl to the corner behind me. Hopefully I'll be too busy chasing these two down to notice you." He smooths my hair and kisses my forehead. "And no matter what you hear, Mariah, don't follow me."

16

MARIAH

The cage door squeals as it swings open. Lilliana
grasps my wrists.

Will is no longer standing beside me, which means he's
returned to his body on the wall—held there now by his
own predatory stillness. I'm still unconscious from the
sedative, but I'm beginning to feel the edges of my
awareness thinning as the drug wears off.

Lilliana steps into the cage, dragging me in after her.
Will's eyes snap open. They're the same impossible
shade of blue they were the night we first met.

"He's awake," Christopher says.

Lilliana looks over her shoulder and sees Will
watching her.

"I don't know how Dad gets so close to that thing,"
Christopher says.

She tugs harder on my arms. "Just shut up and help me
with her legs."

Christopher grasps my ankles. The sound of creaking metal causes them both to freeze in place.

"Is that normal?" Christopher asks.

Lilliana sees the screws on the floor and releases me.

Will's cuffs burst apart as he lunges. Lilliana screams. He's on her, his mouth at her throat, fangs sinking into her neck.

Ripping. Tearing. Shredding.

The sound alone makes me shudder. There's so much blood...

Will crouches over Lilliana's form on the floor, his back heaving as he swallows. Christopher slams the cage door shut. Lilliana cries out to her brother, a garbled call that sounds like she's trying to speak underwater. Blood drips from her mouth. Christopher rips the key from the lock and then fumbles with the keychain, dropping it.

He's trapped me in here with his dying sister and Will's bloodlust.

"No," I say to no one who can hear me.

Christopher flings open the exterior door and disappears into the darkened hall. I kneel by the cage door, looking to see where the keychain fell. It's about an arm's length from the bars. I pour my concentration onto the keychain, willing it to slide toward me, but just as the keys begin to twitch, I feel myself waking up.

I sink back into my body. My head hurts like it's been kicked by a horse. I blink against the light and roll onto my side, coming face to face with Lilliana's open-eyed stare.

"Jesus..." I jerk back. Will has torn a hole in her pants to better reach the artery at her thigh. He looks wilder than an animal, like something pulled straight out of Hell.

Lilliana has stopped crying. If she's not dead already, she's teetering on the edge.

And if I can't get the cage door open, I'll be next.

I crawl on heavy limbs toward the spot where Christopher dropped the keychain. My knees catch on my dress twice, so I bunch the skirt portion up. Reaching through the bars, I stretch my arm as far out as I can.

"Come on," I mutter through clenched teeth, brushing the keys with my fingertips.

A hand grasps my ankle.

I scream. Having mustered her final ounce of strength, Lilliana has grabbed onto me. I meet her pleading gaze with a look of indifference and shake her off. Just minutes ago, she'd been all too eager to watch the same thing happen to me.

It's too late to save her, and even if it wasn't, I wouldn't lift a finger.

Again, I narrow my focus on the ring of keys, calling them into my palm. My heartbeat hammers in my head. Tears stain my cheeks as I work to channel all my effort into drawing them toward me.

An invisible string forms between my hand and the keys.

They slide the extra few inches I need, and then I have them.

I pull myself up and stagger toward the door. The first key I try doesn't work.

A deep, menacing growl makes my skin prickle. Will rises to his feet. I think his color looks better already, but it's hard to tell with the blood smeared all over his face.

"Shit." I try another key, and it turns in the lock. "Thank God..." The door swings inward and I move with it, creating a small cage for myself between the door and the bars behind it.

Will surges, grasping the silver-coated bars in front of me, then draws back, hissing. His hands blister, though I can see his wrists are already healing.

"Will, it's me," I tell him. "It's Mariah. You're free now."

He brings his face close to the bars. I can smell Lilliana's blood all over his mouth.

"Go," I say. "Feed. Make them pay for what they've done to you."

His nostrils flare. He cocks his head, his expression feral, his fangs long and sharp. He's clearly not himself, but a piece of him must still be in there somewhere.

"Please," I whisper, sending waves of calm toward him. "I love you, and I know you love me. Don't do this."

A glimmer of recognition shines in his gaze. Small and fleeting, but strong enough to divert his attention. He turns from me like an ocean liner changing course, stepping out of the cage he's been trapped in for who knows how long.

He sniffs the air. I hold my breath, praying he won't be lured back in my direction by the cut on my wrist. He kicks at the exterior door until it flies off its hinges into the corridor.

As he races off into the darkness, I release my breath and let myself sink onto the concrete.

I count my breaths and wait for the fear to dissipate. But when I close my eyes, all I see is blood. Dripping down walls. Pooling around Lilliana's lifeless body. A vision of Edward loading a silver-tipped bolt into a crossbow.

Of course, I think. The crossbow from Edward's office. He wouldn't keep a vampire in his house without anticipating worst-case scenarios.

I have to warn Will.

Adrenaline pumping, I make my way around Lilliana's corpse. Will warned me not to follow him, but I can't just sit here and allow Edward to kill him. I scan the shelves of medical equipment until I find a roll of gauze and some adhesive. My cut has already begun to coagulate but sneaking up on Will with blood dripping down my arm sounds like a recipe for suicide.

I find a jug of peroxide and pour some over my cut, wincing at the sting. I clean my arm off, then wrap a strip of gauze around my wrist and secure it with tape.

Will's bloody footprints are easy to follow up the stairs. I move quickly and quietly, skittish as a mouse in a house full of cats. The footprints cross each other, but I note a distinct trail leading to the kitchen.

The trail eventually thickens into a smear.

Propping the back door open is Christopher's body—or most of it, at least. I don't notice how unnaturally far his right leg is from the rest of him until I'm standing directly over his corpse. His normally smug face is blank and pale as marble, his neck shredded so badly his head is almost completely separated from his shoulders.

I wonder what it means that I'm not disturbed or horrified by the carnage Will's capable of. Maybe it just hasn't sunk in yet, or maybe I am my father's daughter.

Heartless. Cruel. Detached.

But how can I be heartless if I'm willing to risk my life for the man I love?

A scream pierces the eerie quiet. I race toward the sound, heading in the direction of the foyer. I come upon Will kneeling over Chastity, his fist in her hair and his teeth at her neck.

She sees me, and her face twists in anger. I'm supposed to be dead, but I'm not, and now her son is dead, and Will is free.

It doesn't take a genius to work out the math, and Chastity's hardly a genius.

Will rips a chunk of flesh from her neck. She wails. His tongue snakes out to savor the blood pouring down her chest. He fastens his mouth over the hole in her throat and drinks deeply, as her cries dwindle.

An awareness whispers at my ear. I look up to see Edward at the third-floor railing, aiming his crossbow at Will's back.

He fires.

"No!" I reach out my hand, hurling all of my love and despair toward the silver-tipped bolt.

Will looks up at the sound of my voice. The bolt veers off course and grazes his shoulder. He roars. Tossing Chastity's corpse aside, he turns to glare at Edward. I watch in awe as he leaps to the third-story landing, pulling himself up and over the bannister.

I sprint upstairs, tripping over the hem of my dress. The third time it happens, I rip the skirt part off, sending beads and sequins flying.

When I reach the third story, Edward has his crossbow aimed at Will's chest. Before he can fire off another bolt, Will snatches the weapon out of his hand and hurls it, denting the wall and breaking the bow into pieces.

"Mariah," Edward shouts. "Toss me one of the bolts."

I shake my head. He scowls at me, then cries out as Will grabs him by the shirt collar.

Will swings the top half of Edward's body over the bannister, allowing him to hover. He bares his fangs, tinged red with the blood of Edward's wife and children.

Will opens his mouth, poised to strike. Edward pulls something from his pocket.

I shout for Will to watch out, but Edward is too fast. He sprays something in Will's face that makes him cough and splutter.

He lets go of Edward's collar to rub his eyes.

Edward falls and hits the ground level with a deafening thud.

Will screeches, a furious cry that makes the hairs on my arms stand on end. I approach the bannister slowly, peering over at Edward's prone body below.

A pool of blood spreads outward from the back of his head. His legs are twisted at odd angles.

My father is dead.

I back away from the bannister as the shock I've been outrunning finally catches up to me. I hit what I think is a wall, and then realize is Will's chest. He growls. The sound sends a torrent of fear down my back like tiny pinpricks.

Turning to face him, I'm struck by how large he is. His muscles have filled out. His chest is firm and broad, and he's almost a full head taller than he was in the spirit realm.

My heart beats a drum solo in my chest as I meet Will's gaze. His hunger is unmistakable.

The glint of recognition he felt for me in the cellar is long gone.

He's going to bite me now. He's going to tear into my throat and drink my blood.

He moves toward me, and I feel something hard press into my belly. I glance down, and gasp at the sight of his erect cock, longer and thicker than I remember it being my dream—and even then, it was far above average.

Now that Will's fed, it's like I'm seeing the real him for the first time. A vampire at his most potent.

I'm both terrified and undeniably turned on by the sight of him.

When he used the term *bloodlust* I assumed he was only referring to one type of hunger. But now that his lust for blood has been sated, I suppose that leaves him free to indulge his lust for...other things.

He grabs me by the throat. I whimper as he tows me to the floor, forcing me onto my stomach. His hands move faster than I can register, ripping the back of my dress apart and shredding my panties.

His cock forces its way inside me without difficulty, and I know it's because his whole body is slick with blood. My muscles cry out. I've never had something bigger than my own fingers inside me.

This hurts like nothing I've ever felt before. It's like he's trying to rend me in two.

"Will, please..." He doesn't hear me. He bucks his hips, thrusting in and out of my tender pussy. Hard, fast, and merciless.

I try to crawl away, but he holds me down. The only reprieve I get is when he flips me onto my back. But then, he's back again, rutting into me like a beast. I search his face for a flash of tenderness, some subtle remnant of his love for me.

But all I see reflected at me is heat and hunger.

Tears cloud my vision. His cock slides in at just the right angle, and suddenly I'm hit with something resembling pleasure. My body responds in spite of itself —a defense mechanism, easing my pain by masking it with something better.

I angle my pelvis, hoping he'll hit the same spot again, and he does. I moan. Closing my eyes, I bang on the back door of Will's psyche.

And to my surprise, he lets me in.

Once I'm inside his head, I tap into his pleasure and use it to soothe what's left of my pain. His pleasure becomes my pleasure becomes our pleasure, and soon I'm meeting his thrusts with my own.

He fucks me like a man possessed, like a rabid beast. Like a demon. I sense his bloodlust, the insurmountable need to consume and devour. But I also sense his restraint. He could just as easily have ripped my throat out like he did to the others.

It's his love for me that stops him from doing what comes so naturally to a vampire in his mental state. His bloodlust is something he can't control—just like love itself. Love can be tender and sweet, but it can also be brutal and piercing.

It can draw blood.

On some level, Will knows who I am and that he loves me, but that awareness doesn't reduce his need to consume. It just transforms his hunger from one form to another. And this new hunger still has to take from somewhere, so he's taking his pleasure from me.

His grip on my hips tightens as the need within him climbs. I can feel my orgasm building alongside his. Scratching and clawing its way to the top of the mountain.

We hurl ourselves over the other side, freefalling. He comes, and then I come, piggybacking off his pleasure.

He slams into me, holding me steady. His cock throbs. Warmth spreads outward from the place where our bodies are joined. He growls and I moan, my muscles clenching. His final thrusts are punishing, and I take them. Not just because I'm strong enough, but because in my own perverse way, I enjoy it.

The intensity of his desire, and the pain it brings reminds me that I'm still alive, that Will's alive, and his love for me is stronger than his need for survival.

His fangs graze my shoulder, making me shiver. He licks the spot he just scratched but doesn't bite down. He's returning to himself in the wake of his orgasm. But with renewed awareness comes a deluge of regret.

He knows what he's done to me, and he hates himself for it.

He doesn't know he's already been forgiven.

17

WILLIAM

As the cloud of wrath and hunger dissipates, I realize that I have done something terrible.

There's blood everywhere. All over me and the floor and smeared across the body of the girl in front of me.

Mariah, I remember. Her name is Mariah.

And my cock is still inside her.

No, I think. *Please, no...*

I check her over in a panic, making sure she hasn't been bitten. She's alive, but badly ruffled. Breathing, but dazed. I withdraw from her body, and she lets out the softest whimper. I smell the blood, old and new, theirs as well as hers.

I have done something unforgivable.

An avalanche of regret overtakes me. I press my forehead to her chest. No amount of contrition will ever make up for the damage I have done, but I repent anyway.

"I'm sorry," I tell her, over and over again. "I'm so sorry, my love."

I kiss her face and the bruises on her body, the violet palm prints on her hips. I kiss her pussy gently, like doing so will make it all better. But I can't fix this with a kiss any more than kissing a papercut would make it heal faster.

"Will," she croaks. I move up her body, bracing for the anguish I expect to see reflected at me. But this beautiful, extraordinary creature just smiles at me through her tears. "You're back."

I kiss her forehead. "I'm so sorry."

"You're sad." She touches my cheek. "Don't be sad. We're free."

Free. I choke on the word. The irony that she won't want to be anywhere near me now that we can finally be together almost makes me laugh. I sit up, pulling her into my lap, and begin rocking her gently. She curls up like a cat, her dark head tucked beneath my chin.

"How bad was it?" I ask.

"Pretty bad. There was a ton of blood. Edward fell and then you..."

She trails off, and I want to hurl myself off the balcony right alongside her father.

"Tapping into your pleasure made it feel a lot better," she says.

I figured that's what she was up to. I felt her rooting around in my mind at one point, though I couldn't reach her. "That was a bold and brilliant move. But it doesn't excuse the way I hurt you."

"It could've been worse, Will. A lot worse."

"I didn't know if I could stop myself from..." I can't bring myself to say the words. *Stop myself from killing you.*

"But you did."

"It could just as easily have gone the other way."

"I don't believe that," she says. I cradle her face, brushing my thumb over the dry blood smeared across her cheek.

All week, I've been striving to avoid scenarios that could bring about Katherine's vision of Mariah dying in my arms with her throat torn out. I've never known her visions to be wrong, yet Mariah placed herself well within reach of that fate tonight, and here she is, alive.

It'll be at least a few days before I have to feed again, and I can make damn sure I'm far away from here when the need arises. The safest thing would be for me to leave as soon as possible, but I can't abandon her like this, covered in blood, surrounded by the corpses of her dead relatives.

I can't undo the harm I've caused Mariah, but I can begin to ease her pain.

Now that I've fed, she's as light as a whisper. I gather her up and bring her to one of the nicer guest bathrooms, where I run a bath in the clawfoot tub. I set her in the water and then climb in after. As I lather us both with soap, the water quickly turns pink from all the blood.

I drain the tub and refill it. She sighs with pleasure as I wash the blood from her breasts. I work my way down her body, wishing I could cleanse her memories just as easily. I'm especially careful when tending to her pussy. Still, she flinches at my touch.

"I'm all right," she says. "Really."

"I don't see how that's possible."

"Will, I understand why you feel guilty, but I'm not frightened or traumatized or whatever it is you think I should be."

I want to believe her, but I know forgiveness is too much to ask for, considering what I've already taken. She reorients herself in the water so that she's facing me.

"You love me," she says.

"That doesn't justify what I did to you—"

"You *saved* me. I'd be dead right now if it wasn't for you."

"And I'd still be Edward's prisoner if it wasn't for you."

She smiles. "There. That makes us even."

"Not even close." However, I know one thing that can bring us closer to even. I bite the tip of my forefinger and hold it out to her. "Drink. You'll heal faster."

She frowns. "I'm not like my father, Will. I won't steal your blood for my own benefit."

"You're not stealing anything. I'm offering it to you."

She shakes her head.

"Please, Mariah. It'll hurt less."

"Maybe I don't want it to hurt less." She attempts to pull herself out of the tub and winces. "Okay, fine. But only because the faster I heal, the sooner we can have sex again."

"Yeah, that's not going to happen for a while."

"We'll see." She licks the blood from the tip of my finger.

I draw her to my chest, and she relaxes against me. Within minutes, the purple bruises on her hips begin to fade.

"You know, Will. it's not really up to you, or anyone, to decide how I feel about what happened."

I want to object, but I can tell she's not going to budge on the issue, and perhaps, to an extent, she's right not to. I can't say I fully recall what happened between us after the bloodlust took hold. I expected her to recoil from me as soon as she came to. But she didn't. She stayed.

To presume she couldn't have found a way to manage on her own terms is doubting her resiliency.

And Mariah is the one of the most resilient people I've ever known.

"I'll have to find a wolf or a black bear to pin all this on before the sun comes up," I say.

"Are the cops really going to believe a bear did all that?"

"You could tell them a vampire went on a rampage, but they might bring you in for a psych evaluation. Ideally I'd frame a werewolf, but I assume you don't have one handy."

Her eyes widen. "Werewolves are real?"

"Vampires and ghosts are just the tip of the iceberg, sweetheart."

I towel us off and drain the tub, then carry her to bed. My intention is to let her get some rest, but she reaches for me as I turn to leave her.

"Please stay," she says. "At least until I fall asleep."

I slide under the covers with her, and she curls into my side. Holding her in my arms after everything that's happened feels like a dream. I suspect it will take a while before I accept that this is my new reality.

She skims her fingers over my chest. "You're so much bigger in person," she says quietly.

"Projection takes energy," I tell her. "I rarely had much to spare, so I had to make a few concessions."

"I feel miniature next to you."

"You could be the size of a bird in my palm, and you'd still be one of the bravest creatures I've ever met." I kiss her softly. She stretches out, pressing her body against mine and gliding her hand down my abdomen.

When she finds my cock, I'm hard again and wanting her, but I remind myself how recently I had her pinned to the floor. My thumb brushes her breast as I sweep my hand along her side. She wraps her fingers around my shaft and strokes.

My cock throbs. I want to be inside her and all over her, everywhere at once.

"Are you sure?"

She nods. "It doesn't hurt anymore."

I sense her at the edges of my mind and make space for her to enter. Her presence fills my head. She pours her desire, her love, and her longing into me, until there's no doubt in my mind that this is exactly what she needs right now.

I slide my hand between her legs to stroke her clit. She rocks her hips. She wants more but watching her chase her own pleasure, like a greyhound racing around a track, is a thing of beauty I don't want to miss. I kiss her, and she opens her mouth to greet my tongue, all while her hand continues to jack me to an impossible level of stiffness.

She drapes her leg over my hip. I fuck into her fist, fighting the urge to flip her onto her back and slide home.

Do it. She speaks the words directly into my mind. *It's okay. I want it...*

She doesn't have to tell me twice.

Fitting myself between her legs, I push inside her slowly, the way I should've and no doubt did not do the first time around. She moans. I ease back and glide forward in slow, measured thrusts. She's very wet and very tight, and I feel like a bastard for expecting her to take my unforgiving monster cock into her soft, human body.

But she doesn't just take it. She welcomes it, rearranges her insides to embrace every inch of it.

She wraps herself around me, her body radiating power.

"I love you so much," she whispers.

"I love you, too," I rasp. "I've wanted you from the moment we met, and now you're mine. Say it."

"I'm yours. I'm all yours. I'll *always* be yours."

My fangs extend as they always do when I approach orgasm. She gasps at the sight of them but doesn't scream. She kisses me, caressing the edges of my fangs with the tip of her tongue. She can't know what it means to me that she would embrace the most ferocious parts of me with the softest parts of herself.

The level of trust alone is almost enough to get my still heart pounding again.

I drive into her, pumping steadily. I want her to come. I want to feel her spasm around me, hear the sounds she makes as she breaks apart in my arms. I want my cock to be the reason her toes curl, the thing that makes her eyes roll back inside her head.

Her orgasm swells in my own body, like we're the same person.

I touch my lips to her throat. She senses my desire to taste her, as I would any lover, and fills my head with a sense of rightness, of permission.

She gasps as my fangs pierce her skin at the moment her pleasure starts to crest. She's beyond delicious. I draw from her, just enough to fill my mouth, and the pleasure I gain from the intimate exchange radiates outward, into her, and back, like a current. I push into her, hard. Harder than I have any right to, and she meets me, thrust for thrust.

We crescendo together, straining and releasing. Grasping and holding.

I refuse to pull out, even when it's over. I don't want to lose this feeling of being buried inside the girl I love. This is the closest I've come to feeling anywhere close to home, which is something I never expected to feel inside these walls.

Mariah runs her hands up and down my back.

"Thank you," she whispers.

I lift my head to look at her. "For what?"

"Not treating me like glass."

I kiss her. She licks her own blood from her lips with a curious expression.

"You know," she says, "blood actually goes kind of well with red velvet cake."

I'm suddenly reminded what today is—or was. I check the clock on the nightstand. It's a little after one in the morning.

"Happy belated birthday," I tell her. "I'm sorry I wasn't able to get you a present."

"You mean, besides the two orgasms and my family's ancestral estate that will probably be left to me, as my father's sole living heir?"

"Besides all that, yes." I eye her with interest. "Two orgasms?"

She bites her smiling lips. "Like I said, the first time wasn't all bad."

I shake my head in amazement. My inner demon has finally met his match.

"I'm sorry you weren't able to get revenge on my father," she says. "I guess the important thing is that he's dead, but I'm sure you wanted to be the one to kill him. What was that stuff he sprayed in your face?"

"Colloidal silver. It's like mace for vampires." I stroke her flushed cheek. "I would've liked to have killed Edward with my own fangs, but what I have in front of me is more important and more precious than revenge. Doubting my love for you is my greatest regret. More than placing my trust in your father. I was convinced I would kill you if given the chance. I should've trusted us. Trusted myself, with you."

"I'm sorry I didn't believe you. I could've freed you sooner."

"Everything happened as it was meant to," I tell her.

Katherine must've been mistaken. I could never harm Mariah. I begin to move inside her again, and she moans, opening for me, her body already a slave to its adoring master. In all my five hundred years, I've never known a woman I didn't think I could eventually say goodbye to.

Trying to imagine a future without Mariah is like picturing a sunset sapped of color.

Before Mariah, all I knew was pain and rage and darkness. Then she appeared on the horizon, more beautiful than sunlight. She was a burst of fire across my charcoal sky.

The sunset wouldn't be the same without her, and neither would I.

18

MARIAH

I awaken in the grass outside the main house to the clamor of swing music and clinking glasses. After all the carnage I've witnessed, I'm glad to see the ghosts are still having a good time. However, I'm decidedly not in the partying mood, so I make my way out to the field, running my hands along the tops of the vine rows as I go.

Will isn't here, but I don't expect him to be. Now that he's free, he doesn't need to escape to the spirit world to be with me. He can simply pull me closer.

Someone whispers my name. I turn in the direction of the sound. A mist rolls through the field, a thick, white cloud as high as my waist, carrying voices.

He's coming... He's coming... He's here...

A shadow falls over the vineyard. I feel its presence. Cold. Dense. Menacing. I yelp as someone grips my shoulders and turns me around, bringing me face to face with my mother.

"Wake up, baby." She snaps her fingers.

I startle awake in bed. It's nighttime, possibly very early morning. My chest feels tight. I cough. The evil presence I felt in the spirit realm is still here, curling around me like smoke. I reach for Will, but his side of the bed is empty. Then I recall him mentioning something about going to find a bear before dawn.

Pulling the covers back, I pivot to climb out of bed—and then rear back as a figure emerges from the shadows.

"You disappoint me, Mariah," Edward says, his eyes glowing like embers in the dark. "I had such high hopes for what we might accomplish together."

I swallow the lump of fear in my throat like a bitter pill. "I saw you fall, Edward. I watched you die."

"You did," he says. "But I have been reborn."

He moves toward the bed. I attempt to scurry away from him, but he grabs my ankle. His grip is like iron. I'm as vulnerable as it gets, naked without a weapon. I flinch as he reaches out to pinch a lock of my hair between his fingertips.

"I see now that this is how it was always meant to be," he says. "A human can only gain so much from drinking vampire blood. But a vampire possesses infinite power, so long as he's well fed."

Fear tightens its hold on me, as I gaze into those floating red embers.

My father is a vampire, I realize.

And I'm the only living human in the house.

"I understand how William got to you," he says. "How he turned you against me. Sadly, your powers are lost to me now. But your blood can still be of use."

He lunges, pushing me down on the bed. I slap and kick and shove, but it's like trying to fight off a rockslide with your bare hands.

Pain explodes in my neck as he sinks his fangs into me. I scream, but the sound is cut off by blood flooding my throat. It fills my mouth. Everything is happening at once, and yet I feel every second of it, as though the last remaining minutes of my life are being played out in slow motion.

My attention fades as fatigue sets in. I attempt to call out to Will with my mind before darkness overtakes me.

I'm too late.

I come to on the floor in the conservatory. My mother is here, holding out her hand.

"Come on, baby," she says. "We have to hurry."

My grandmother appears. They each take one of my hands, and the three of us start running. Through the foyer, up the stairs, down the hall to where Edward crouches over my body.

The wet, gurgling sounds of his feeding make me nauseous. I glance down at my own face, at the life quickly draining from my eyes.

"You can stop him," my grandmother says. "Use your gifts."

I take a breath and work to channel my focus into Edward's mind. He shakes me off like a fly.

"Get closer," my mother says.

Climbing onto the bed, I hold my hands to either side of Edward's head and try again. It's a monumental effort to concentrate. With each passing second, it feels like more and more of me is being lost down a long, dark drain.

Hands rest upon my shoulders. My mother and grandmother standing to the left and right of me, lending me their strength. I clench my jaw and concentrate on infiltrating Edward's mind.

Centering. Tunneling. Delving inside...

My palms start to burn. I recall the pain I felt as his fangs ripped into my neck and roll that sensation into a ball that I then hurl at him.

Edward lets out an ear-splitting screech. He lifts his face from my throat, and I move with him, fighting to maintain the connection I've established. I condense my own pain and anguish into agony that I channel his way.

"That's it, Mariah," my mom says. "Now finish it."

My hands glow as heat courses through them. I grasp the sides of Edward's head. Finally, he sees me, his expression twisting in disbelief. I hold his gaze as I give him the full force of my concentration, screaming in his face.

Milky blood seeps from the corners of his eyes, mouth, and nose. A bright light blinds me. I tumble backward onto the floor as Edward collapses. I can't feel his presence anymore.

Then again, I'm having trouble feeling much of anything.

Will comes careening into the room, his gaze wild. He sees Edward and then me—on the bed as well as the floor.

"No," he says, glancing between both versions of me, not sure which one to run to.

In a flurry of movement, he grabs Edward's head and rips it off his shoulders, then shoves my father's disparate parts to the floor. He cradles my body in his lap on the bed.

"I can't lose you like this," he says over me. "Not to him."

I sway in place. Everything hurts, yet so much of me is already gone.

"How did he come back?" I ask.

"He must've drank my venom last night when he realized I was coming for him," Will says, glowering at the heaps of meat on the floor. "This was his insurance policy."

"She doesn't have much time, William," my grandmother says. "Make your choice."

He scowls. "What choice is that, Katherine? You already know what's going to happen, so why don't you just fucking tell me."

"Will?" I feel my edges fading. He reaches for me, and I fall straight through his hands—back into my body.

I cough and splutter. My vision is blurred, like somebody's placed a strip of gauze over my eyes. Will presses his forehead to mine.

"Listen to me, Mariah. If I drain you fully, you'll die and become a ghost. But if I let you die with Edward's venom in your system, there's a chance you'll come back...like me. You have to tell me what you want, or I'm going to choose for you, and it's going to be a selfish choice, because I'd rather you hate me forever as a vampire than be forced to live without you."

What's left of me is fast slipping away, like the last few grains of sand in the neck of an hourglass. Becoming a vampire wouldn't just mean turning it over. It would mean shattering the hourglass completely and tossing the shards into the desert.

Infinite grains of sand as far as the eye can see.

Will's right about it being no choice at all. My fate was sealed the moment we met in the vineyard.

"Let me die," I whisper.

And then, I'm gone.

19

MARIAH

I dream that I am small. Maybe five or six years old. Sitting on my grandpa's shoulders. We're at Assateague State Park with my mom and her friend Kim. I squeal excitedly as a brown-and-black pony clomps across the packed sand. I ask where Will is, but nobody hears me. I ask again, where's Will? They tell me he's not here yet, and I start to cry.

I dream that I'm fourteen, getting my braces removed. My teeth feel like a string of pearls when I run my tongue over them. The dental hygenist hands me a mirror and I smile at my reflection. Then I notice that my teeth are all sharp, each one capped with a fang. My lips are bleeding. So is my tongue. I ask the hygienist if Will is here yet, and she says no.

I dream that it's prom night. I never went to prom, so I know I'm dreaming. Plus, I'm wearing the red beaded dress Edward gave me for my birthday. My boyfriend—who happens to look just like Zack Morris from *Saved by the Bell*—is trying to convince me to go all the way with him tonight. I tell him I'm waiting. He asks what I'm waiting for, and I say, I'm waiting for Will.

All this time, I've been waiting for Will.

Now he waits for me.

20

MARIAH

D ying isn't the hard part. It's coming back to life that's the real bitch. I'm there for all of it, every millisecond my body spends repairing itself, building itself anew.

Stronger. Faster. More powerful.

I feel about a thousand years old by the time I'm ready to open my eyes again.

The room I'm in is familiar. Yellow walls, white linens, a big armoire in the corner. It looks like my mom's room in the guesthouse, but the furniture is arranged differently.

Will is seated in a chair beside the bed with his eyes closed. My mother sits at the foot of my bed.

"He's looking for you in the twilight realm," my mom says. "He wants to be there to greet you in case your transition failed."

I'm quite certain the transition didn't fail. My canines feel sharper, though they aren't long and terrifying like Will's were in the midst of his bloodlust. Maybe that only happens when a vampire is turned on, or hungry. I have so much to learn about my new self.

I sit upright to stretch. Someone—most likely Will— has dressed me in my mom's old Fleetwood Mac tee shirt.

I reach for my mother's hand and my fingers pass through her.

"You're corporeal," she says. "We'll have to save the hugs for when you're projecting."

I reach over to touch Will's face, but he doesn't stir. He must be in deep.

"Do I have to wait till I'm asleep, or do you think I can learn to project while awake?"

"I doubt becoming a vampire has made your gifts *weaker*," she says. "You could test it out."

Closing my eyes, I picture myself rising out of my body, light as air. I soar over trees and roads, until I find myself in front of the estate.

Suddenly, I'm there.

I take off into the field in search of Will. When I find him, it's in the same spot where I first met him, standing among the vines, facing the horizon.

"Hello," I say.

He turns around, the brightness of his smile dulled by sadness.

"Hello, there," he says. He thinks I'm a ghost.

I run and jump, leaping over trellises. He grunts softly as I tackle him to the ground, shocked to find me solid.

"How's this possible?" he asks.

I kiss him, moaning softly as he folds his arms around me.

"Anything is possible in a dream," I tell him.

We return to the physical realm at the same time. As soon as he's back in control of himself, he rises from the chair to embrace me.

"You made it," he says, smoothing my hair back from my face. "I knew you'd make it. And holy hell, you are beautiful."

I haven't seen my reflection, so I have no idea if I look any different as a vampire. From the way he's gazing at me, I don't think my appearance suffered at all from the transition.

"I'm happy to see you, too."

He kisses me like we're the only two people left in the universe.

Somebody clears their throat.

"The police are really itching to get in here and talk to you," my grandpa says.

"Police?" I ask Will.

"I brought you to the guesthouse because I knew the staff would show up in the morning and call the cops. I didn't want them to disturb you during your transition. You'll have to talk to them soon, but I'll be there. They think I'm your fiancé."

"Do they now?" I smile at him. "Whatever gave them that idea?"

Will grins. I allow myself a moment to imagine Will tearing off my wedding dress with his teeth, at least until a more pressing matter arises.

I'm not exactly sure how I killed Edward. An autopsy might raise questions we'd rather not answer. "Did they find Edward's body?"

"Only his body." My grandmother smirks. "His head has mysteriously gone missing."

"What happened to it?" I ask.

Will shrugs. "Guess the bear ate it."

"To put it plainly, sweetheart," my mom says, "you turned his brain to scrambled eggs."

"Oh," I say, a little stunned, but also kind of impressed.

"You did good," my grandpa says with a wink.

Will kisses my brow and then leaves the room. He returns a moment later holding a glass of what looks like blood, which he offers to me. "You need to drink this before we talk to anyone with a pulse."

"What is it?"

"Bear blood. I siphoned some off while I was staging the crime scene."

I take a sip and immediately gag. "That's disgusting."

"I know," Will says. "But this and the bagged stuff in the fridge will tide us over till we can find a ring of child murderers to hunt."

Steeling myself, I gulp down the remainder of the bear blood, preferring the awful taste to the alternative of massacring a bunch of cops and crime-scene investigators in broad daylight.

Speaking of daylight...

"How can we go outside during the day?"

Will chuckles. "Ah, yes, the old bursting into flames in the sun mythos. Thankfully, that's one bit of lore Hollywood gets wrong. The sun burns us at a faster rate, and you'd be in very bad shape if you stood outside for an hour on a bright day, but it won't kill you."

"So, that means I can still catch the occasional sunset?"

Will kisses the back of my hand. "You have infinite sunrises and sunsets ahead of you, my love."

A knock sounds on the front door. Will hands me a pair of jeans he must've grabbed from my room and goes to answer. I get dressed while he stalls the detectives who sound very eager to speak with me.

"Just get through the next few days and it'll all work itself out," my grandmother says. I nod, thanking her for the encouragement, and for all her help, before heading outside to meet the detectives.

The sun feels like bathwater washing over my skin. I'm aware of every wisp of wind, every individual bird call. I smell the papercut on the tall detective's right forefinger and hear the blood pumping through his veins.

Will takes my hand and squeezes it reassuringly.

"We were here together all night," he says. "I'm just grateful we decided not to sleep in the main house. Such a terrible tragedy."

"Ms. Greyson," the short, round, balding detective says. "Can you corroborate your fiancé's whereabouts during last night's animal attack?"

"Absolutely." I meet Will's tender gaze. "He never left my side."

Epilogue

William

One year later...

Mariah's attorney withdraws a stack of papers from his briefcase and sets them on the glass table in front of her. I stand off to the side, among the plants in the conservatory, watching. Making sure she's safe.

Not that she needs my help with that these days.

"Once again, Mrs. Durant," the lawyer says, "I am terribly sorry about what happened to your family. I can't begin to imagine what this year has been like for you."

"It was an ordeal," she says calmly. "But we've managed."

He hands her a pen and shows her where to sign and initial. "Out of curiosity, what do you intend to do with the vineyard now that it's yours?"

"We're reverting some of the fields back to pasture and building a new horse barn."

Both the vineyard and the estate sat in probate for almost a year following the tragedy at Red Cliff, during which time Mariah and I stayed at her old house in Baltimore. She showed me where she went to school, the record store where she once worked. We fucked in her childhood bedroom, surrounded by posters of her favorite bands, more times than I can recall.

Hunting was easier in the city. More people, more crime, less scrutiny. Mariah only gave into her bloodlust once. That was a long and grueling night for both of us. I had to hold her down for five straight hours to stop her from massacring an entire clinic full of people.

That was also the night I gave her one of the most intense orgasms of her life.

My cock perks up every time I think about it.

Baltimore was a fun diversion, but it wasn't home. We knew we would return to Red Cliff, now the Greyson Estate, as soon as the dust had settled.

The house stood empty for months. The vineyard shut down. When we got back, one of the first things Mariah did was change out the dead plants in the conservatory for live ones.

The first thing I did was make her my wife.

We married in the twilight realm, with Katherine officiating. The ghosts were more than happy to celebrate with us. Mariah and I danced and made love for days following the service. After which, I took her hunting on Virginia Beach.

I reached out to an old vampire contact who helped me regain access to my wealth. We hired new staff, including a farm manager, and set about transforming the property into the horse ranch of Mariah's dreams.

The only unfortunate thing about coming home is occasionally running into Chastity and her children. Thankfully, with Isabella and Katherine on watch, they almost never come into the house. One of the most satisfying exchanges I've yet to witness involved Isabella whispering something to the doorman, after which, he informed the Radcliffs, "I'm afraid your invitation to this soiree has been rescinded. Please escort yourselves *off* the premises."

Edward has yet to make an appearance on the estate. Disposing of his head a great distance from his body seems to have trapped him in some kind of spiritual limbo.

I hope, wherever he is, he's wrapped in chains.

Mariah and her attorney finish up their business in the conservatory and say their farewells. As soon as he's gone, she pretends to faint onto the chaise lounge.

"Why didn't you tell me being immortal would involve so much paperwork?"

"Darling, I knew if I told you, you would've asked me to make you a ghost." I lift her into my arms and kiss her, sliding my hand into her back pockets. She rocks against me, humming with pleasure.

Just like that, I want her again.

In fact, I'm quite certain I've never stopped.

"Wait," she says. "You promised we'd watch the sunset."

"I can multitask." She laughs, batting my hands away from her breasts, and then saunters outside knowing I'll follow her.

We make our way across the overgrown field, now free of vines and trellises, to our favorite hill. Someday soon there'll be live horses out here among the dead ones.

We sit in the grass. Mariah leans into me, and I hold her to my chest. After a short while, she says, "I'm going to say hi."

"Go on," I tell her. "I'll join you in a minute."

She walks over to where the horses are grazing. They look up, and a couple even flick their tails at her approach. They know us now. I dare say a few even missed us while we were away.

Isabella appears on the edge of the field, like an eraser acting in reverse, becoming more and more solid with every step. Mariah smiles, happy to see her. They walk together and talk. As I watch them, I find myself thinking about how far we've all come.

I feel Katherine's presence manifest in the grass beside me.

"I suppose I owe you an apology," she says. "Though, to be fair, what I saw did come to pass. I just didn't see that it was Edward who'd bitten her."

"Is that part of your apology? Because it sucks."

She shoots me a look that says *don't push it.*

Isabella climbs onto a horse and trots circles around her daughter. Mariah laughs, spinning in place. I'm sure she's tempted to project herself into the twilight realm so she can ride, too, but then she'd have to miss out on the sunset.

"I am sorry, William," Katherine says. "I was wrong about you."

"Apology accepted."

"That's it?" Katherine scoffs. "No wise cracks or subtle digs? I've waited a year to say that to you. You've made it too damn easy."

"Life's too short to hold grudges, Katherine."

"Says the man who's going to live forever."

"I doubt I'll live forever," I say with a smile. "But watching the woman you love bleed to death puts a lot of things in perspective."

I get up and join Mariah and her mother just as the show's about to begin. Wrapping my arm around Mariah's waist, I turn her in the direction of the setting sun.

The sky catches fire. Clouds glow like cinders, burning orange and magenta. Mariah melts against me, and I hold her up.

I will *always* hold her up.

Long after the fire in the sky burns out, and the darkness comes to claim us.

PLAYLIST

The following playlist served as creative inspiration
throughout the writing of *Blood and Wine*.

"The Power of Love" by Celine Dion

"Dreams" by The Cranberries

"No Rain" by Blind Melon

"Hold On" by Wilson Phillips

"Come As You Are" by Nirvana

"Dreamlover" by Mariah Carey

"Kiss From a Rose" by Seal

"Damn I Wish I Was Your Lover" by Sophie B. Hawkins

"Closer" by Nine Inch Nails

"Come To My Window" by Melissa Ethridge

"Lovesong" by The Cure

"Angel" by Aerosmith

"Landslide" by Fleetwood Mac

"Rain" by Madonna

"I Have Nothing" by Whitney Houston

About Margot

 Margot Scott likes long nails and short, sexy reads, rainbow sprinkles on vanilla ice cream, and rainy days spent in bed with her furbabies. When she's not writing forbidden love stories about bearded older men, you can find her browsing Pinterest for pictures of pink things.

Visit margotscott.com to learn more.

Printed in Great Britain
by Amazon

23246458R00108